A BOSS' LOVE SAVED MY HEART

DEEANN
AJ DIX

D1528714

TEXT UCP TO 22828 TO SUBSCRIBE TO OUR MAILING LIST
If you would like to join our team, submit the first 3-4 chapters of your completed manuscript to
Submissions@UrbanChapterspublications.com

CONNECT WITH DEEANN:

Facebook 'Personal' Page: Dee Ann
Facebook 'Like' Page: DeeAnn
Reading group: DeeAnn's Readers Den
Twitter: @AuthorDeeAnn_
Instagram: @iam_deeann
Email: authoressdeeann@yahoo.com
Website: iamdeeann.com

CONNECT WITH AJ DIX

Facebook 'personal page': AJ Dix
Facebook 'like' page: Authoress AJ Dix
Instagram: ashley_jovan
Twitter: bunniepjs
Readers group:
https://www.facebook.com/groups/1848207391862436/?
ref=bookmarks

1

SAMEERAH

"Meeraaahhh! Leggo, bitch! I'm ready to shake this fat ass all around those fine ass fraternity niggas and they bitches!" my best friend, Leikyn yelled from her bathroom.

Rolling my eyes, I laid back on her bed and wished she would just go without me. I didn't feel like partying tonight when I had an exam tomorrow. Hell, her ass did too, so we both needed to be studying. Instead, Lei's fast ass wanted to go out and be all up in the mix. I was somewhat antisocial, so I didn't care to be around all the loud, obnoxious music, drunk freshmen, and weed smoke. I wanted peace, but I knew Lei wouldn't allow me to have it.

"SAMEERAH!" she snapped when she barged in the room and saw me laid out. I giggled and groaned.

"Lei, why can't you go out by yourself? I'm tired. I need to study. *We* need to study," I emphasized, scowling her. She kissed her teeth and rolled her eyes.

"Your ass been studying for this shit for two weeks. You should know it by heart because I damn sure do. I don't even

1

know why you act like that, Meerah. We go through this shit almost every time I ask you to go out with me."

"So, why do you keep asking me?"

"Because you need to loosen the fuck up and get some dick or something. I love you, but you're too fuckin' uptight. Anytime we go out, we *always* leave early because you're complaining, or Taizere bum ass call, needing you. I'm not letting you ruin shit tonight."

"First of all, I do get dick. Taizere fills me up any chance he gets. Second, don't call my baby a bum, Lei. You know he's trying."

"Yeah, trying to drain what little you have in your damn pockets," she mumbled, holding hands up in surrender. "I'm going to let that subject go because we won't get anywhere with it. Now, get off your ass and come on. I'm almost ready."

I watched Lei switch away in her skin-tight jumpsuit. I couldn't lie, it was cute as hell and fit her curvy body just right. Lei stood at about 5'7" with long, thick legs and nice, robust ass.

She knew she was bad and loved showing off what she had. Her skin was painted the color of milky cocoa with heart-shaped, thick lips, slender nose, and deep-set expresso colored eyes. Not only was her body hitting, but she was gorgeous. Many females envied her because she wasn't just looks, but smart as a wiz, too. We both were.

Lei and I had been best friends since high school. We went to the same school but grew up in two totally different neighborhoods. While Lei and her family lived in the suburbs, I grew up in the hood with my crack-addicted mother. Lei had a silver spoon while I struggled to keep a plastic one. We lived in two different worlds, but that never stopped us from being friends. She knew my struggle and did whatever she could to help me through. When I didn't have the money to pay for my school uniform and school supplies, her parents handled it for me. My mama would get upset about me taking things from them, but I didn't know what else to do.

I got tired of stealing, and she used all the money she got for crack. I had no choice, and I was thankful they thought enough of me to care about my well-being. Unlike her.

Allow me to introduce myself. I'm Sameerah Wagner and I'm twenty-one years old. I was born and raised in Atlanta, GA with no plans of ever leaving.

Atlanta was considered "Black Hollywood," and I wanted to stay amongst my kind. I attended Clark University where I was majoring in Management on a full four-year scholarship. With only a year left to go, I couldn't wait to finish and head on to my Masters. Growing up with nothing, I had goals to get everything I ever wanted. That's why I prided myself in going hard in school and staying on top. By the time I graduated, I had plans to have a job waiting for me to get with my degree in hand or open my own business. I would be fine with either.

I was the only child born to a crack-addicted woman. She stopped long enough to ensure I was born healthy, but after she pushed me out, she went right back to it. Honestly, I had been caring for myself since I was a small child. Not only did I take care of myself, but often, I had to take care of my mother as well. She would be too high to function, and I hated seeing her so messed up. I did what I could for her because she was my mother and I loved her. Countless times, I prayed to God that He would knock that demon off her back. It's going on twenty-two plus years and she was still fighting it.

I had given up hope she would beat it. Every day, I waited for the call from someone telling me she had overdosed. Sad, but true.

I knew I wouldn't win tonight with Leikyn, so I dragged

my feet over to the mirror to check my appearance. I felt so uncomfortable in what I wore. Leikyn insisted I try something new, but I wasn't feeling it. She went out and bought us matching jumpsuits. The only difference was mine was red and hers was white. I loved the way it made my slim frame look as if I had more curves than what I did. I didn't have anything on Lei, but I had enough to turn heads.

The red complimented my smooth, blemish-free, Nutella colored skin. My hair was slightly curled with a middle part. I felt middle parts went well with my narrow face and high cheekbones. My nose was slightly pointed, and my lips were average but plump. Pleased with my look, I snapped a quick picture and debated on posting it on social media.

"SAMEERAH!"

"I'M COMING, LEI!"

"Girl, I'm so ready," she squealed, twerking while she drove. "I got us both a small bottle of D'usse to get us right. You're taking at least a shot, Meerah. I'm not taking no for an answer."

"Whatever. If it shuts you up."

My phone chimed, and it was Taizere texting asking where I was. Taizere and I had been together for three years. I met him my freshman year of college at a house party Lei dragged me to, and we had been tight ever since. Taizere was in the process of becoming a rapper. He moved to Atlanta from Mississippi to try and get his career off the ground. It was a struggle, but I was proud of him for not giving up.

On top of caring for my mother, I helped Taizere out too. He used most of his money on studio time and other shit, leaving me to help pick up what he couldn't handle on his own. I didn't have a lot of money, so I did what I could. I would have more if it wasn't for the two people I loved most.

Kissing my teeth, I read his text and locked my phone. I was livid. He had used the money I had stashed for our light bill for studio time. The light bill was due in a few days, and now, I had to think of how to get the money for it. My savings was getting low, so I tried to avoid using any money from it, but I would probably have to.

"Where's my bottle?" I grumbled, searching around for it. When I found the brown bag, I didn't waste time opening my bottle and taking two big gulps. I welcomed the burn in my throat and sting in my eyes. The way I felt, I was liable to drink the entire bottle.

"Damn, bitch! Wait on me to turn up like that. What's gotten into you?" Lei asked. I gave her a look, and she nodded. I silently thanked her for not chastising me about him. She let me have my moment.

By the time we pulled up to the party, I was feeling good. I no longer cared about studying and enjoyed the vibe of the party. It was lit. Niggas were everywhere, literally. I got excited when they started stepping. That was one thing I did love about the parties when I attended. They always put on a good show.

The one thing I hated about it, it was packed as hell. I hated touching other people. Other sweaty people.

Cardi B's, *She Bad* filled the room and all the girls went wild. When Leikyn started twerking, it made all the girls around envious. I giggled as they stared daggers at her while the men drooled. A circle had formed around her. Not usually the one to interact, the liquor had me acting as her personal hype man. The more I hyped her, the harder she twerked. All the fun was interrupted when some nigga came and yanked her up by her arm.

"Take yo' ass to the car, bruh. The fuck you out here shakin' ya' ass for in front of these niggas?" he barked, yelling at her back.

The crowd dispersed, and everyone went back to their own worlds. Stumbling, I took my heels off and went outside.

My vision was a little blurry, but I was able to spot Lei and the guy walking down the sidewalk. Careful not to fall, I jogged until I caught up with them. They were yelling back and forth, but I had never seen Lei back down from anyone like she did him.

"You need something?" he asked me, irritated. Lei smacked her lips.

"Levi, this is Sameerah. My best friend I'm always telling you about," she explained, introducing us.

Levi. It was her brother. He had been in California for the past few years doing business. I didn't expect to see him here, and I didn't expect him to be so fine. Pictures didn't do him any justice.

Levi was on the shorter side, about an inch taller than Lei. They shared the same Hershey skin, nose and lips. He had a full, unkempt beard that was sexy in some odd way. Diamonds rested in his ears, along with his other jewelry. It wasn't flashy, but noticeable. When he licked his lips, my knees buckled. It was something about him.

"You were in there bein' hoeish with my sister?"

"Excuse me?"

"You hard of hearin', bruh? I know you heard me, Lil' Black Girl."

"Meerah, ignore his rude ass. Come on. I'm ready to go now," Lei pouted, walking away. I followed behind her and Levi was hot on our heels. He waited until we were in the car and drove off before walking in the other direction.

"I can't stand his ass," Lei mumbled.

"I thought he lived in Cali?"

"He does, but I forgot he said he was coming to visit. He didn't tell me when, like always. His ass just popped up and embarrassed the fuck out of me. I'm gon' have to lay low for at least two weeks."

"Yeah, he didn't have to jack you up like that. I'm embarrassed for you."

"Girl, I'm over it. I'm about to take my ass home and see what nigga wants to come over. You coming with me or am I taking you home?"

"Take me home. I don't have my books with me."

Lei took me home and we made plans to meet up before our class to go over notes. She promised to text me when she got home. I went inside to an empty apartment. Taizere was probably at the studio or club, and I was fine with that. I didn't feel like being bothered with him anyways.

I washed my makeup off and climbed in the shower. Visions of Levi flashed across my mind. I couldn't help but wonder when I would see him again. Probably never. Shaking those feelings off, I finished my shower and studied a little before I fell asleep with my notes in hand.

2

LEIKYN

After dropping Sameerah off at home, I *was* going to go home too, but I thought about how this nigga had me fucked up and went in the opposite direction. It took me fifteen minutes to get to my destination, and I hopped out on a mission. With my purse in one hand, I stomped up to the door and banged on it like I was the police. After standing there for a minute too long, I turned and used my foot to bang a little louder.

Boom! Boom! Boom!

"Yo what the fuck?" Micah snatched the door open, and I had to stop myself from drooling at how sexy he was looking shirtless, with his dreads swinging past his shoulders.

"That's what the I'm trying to figure out, Micah. What the fuck?" I pushed past him and walked inside his house. I threw my purse on his couch and turned to face him with my arms folded across my chest.

"What's wrong now, Lei Lei?" Micah sighed and walked to the kitchen.

I was right on his heels. "Don't *Lei Lei* me. Why didn't I

know that you and my big head brother was coming in town today?"

"Shit, that's your brother, I thought he would've told you."

"And you're my— you know what, never mind," I huffed in annoyance. I tried to storm off, but Micah wrapped his arm around my waist and pulled me into his chest.

"Why you come in here blanking like that? If you missed me that's all you had to say," Micah whispered with his cool breath tickling my ear. When his lips brushed across my neck, my knees got weak as I melted into his arms.

"Let me go, I ain't messin' with you," I lied. I was trying to keep this attitude going, but my body was betraying me.

"Why you lying to yourself? I know you ain't drive all the way over here to be mad," Micah called me out.

He was right; I didn't come over here to talk or be mad. I wanted him to spread me all across his apartment and fuck me silly. But he didn't know that. Micah turned me around and wasted no time pressing his lips into mine. I welcomed his tongue into my mouth and sucked on it a little before letting go. I could taste the weed on his tongue, but I didn't care at this moment. He picked me up and I wrapped my legs around his waist as he walked us to the couch. I'm not a little bitch, and I love when Micah would toss me around and show me he was all man.

"I'm not even gon' say nothing about this tight shit you wearing. But you know better," Micah said in between kisses as he unzipped my jumpsuit. Just as he popped a nipple in his mouth, his phone started going off in his pocket.

"Don't answer that," I moaned out, enjoying what he was doing to my body.

"I got to. Watch out, baby girl." He tapped my ass so I could lift up, and he pulled his phone out. "Yo? Naw, I'm chillin' tonight. Nah, I don't know about all that."

No, this nigga didn't, I thought as I got up out his lap and forcibly zipped my jumpsuit back up. I could clearly hear a bitch's voice on the other end of that phone. I don't know why Micah wanted to play like I wouldn't turn his entire fuckin' house upside down.

"Where you going?" Micah questioned me.

"Home before I end up fuckin' you up in here," I mumbled.

"For what?" This nigga was sitting here looking confused like he really didn't know what was up.

"You gon' answer the phone for some hoe like I'm not sitting here. Who was that?" I know I didn't want to know because I'll wind up trying to find whoever she is.

"You ain't got that right to be questioning me, ma. I'm single."

It felt like I was donkey kicked in my stomach when he said that. All I could reply was, "Bet."

"You the one said that you don't do long-distance relationships, remember? Don't get mad when I give you what you ask for." Micah nonchalantly shrugged his shoulders, further pissing me off.

"Fuck you, nigga!" I snatched my purse up and stormed out the house, leaving his door wide open.

"Petty ass!" I heard him yell out before slamming his door.

I did eighty all the way home, ignoring every call from Micah. I was tipsy, pissed, and horny, and wasn't in the mood for his shit anymore.

Let me give y'all a little back story on me and Micah. Micah is my brother Levi's best friend, so we pretty much grew up around each other. When my body started to mature, and I start smelling myself, as my granny says, that's when my infatuation with Micah started.

Micah is five years older than me and always treated me like an annoying little sister. I hated it. It wasn't until my eighteenth birthday that he took my advances serious. We started kickin' it heavy, and he was even the first guy to get my sacred kitty. I wanted to keep whatever we were doing a secret from Levi, and he agreed. Everything was going good until Levi and Micah popped up talking about they were moving to California. My heart was broken and when they left, I didn't talk to him for a few months. It took Micah popping up at my house and fuckin' me silly to break the ice between us. Micah promised to visit more, so every couple of weeks, he'll pop up, make me fall in love all over again, and go back to Cali until the next time. I was starting to feel like I was wasting the best years of my damn life, but I couldn't leave that man alone to save my life.

Me: I'm home, bestie. Love you!

I sent the text off to Sameerah, knowing she was probably already sleeping. My best friend acted like she was a little old woman sometimes and not twenty-one years old. If she wasn't in school, she was at home with that tired ass boyfriend of hers. I thought I was going to have to drag her out tonight, but I was happy she obliged. I had some more parties for us to hit up this weekend, and I wasn't taking no for an answer from her.

After showering, I laid across my bed naked as the day I came into this world. I hated sleeping with clothes on. It took me no time at all to fall into a deep slumber.

The next morning, I was wakened up to my phone ringing like crazy.

"What?" I groaned into the phone.

"Um, get yo' ass up before you be late to class," Sameerah fussed.

Hearing that had my eyes popping open and checking the time. "Shit," I cursed. I had a little under an hour to get dressed and make it to class on time. "I'm up and getting ready now." I quickly hung up and ran to my bathroom to handle my hygiene.

I didn't have time to get all dolled up like I usually did, so I just got dressed in a crop top, and some distressed jeans. I threw my hair up in a slick ponytail and put my gloss on my lips. After grabbing what I needed for class, I left to go pick up Sameerah. Since we were in the same class, we always rode together.

When I pulled up to her house, Taizere was on his way out. He gave me a head nod, and I just looked at him blankly. I didn't have anything personal against Taizere, except for him being a bum, and not good enough for my best friend. I wanted to be petty and ask how come I ain't heard his shit on the radio yet. But I knew if he got out of line, Levi would have to put him back, and nobody wanted that.

"Hey babe," Sameerah greeted as she got in the passenger seat, smiling.

"How are you so energetic this morning? I'm ready to climb back in my bed for a couple more hours," I groaned as I pulled off.

"Well, you shouldn't have been up all night thottin'," she laughed.

"Girl, I wish I would've got some dick last night." I rolled my eyes thinking about the encounter with Micah last night. Just thinking about it had me ready to call and cuss his ass out again.

We arrived at school and went right to class since we were behind schedule. The instructor was already there passing out the exams. Me and Sameerah grabbed our tests and took our seats in the back as always.

It took no time to finish the test before we were on our way back out the door. This was our only Friday class and I was happy because we had the rest of the weekend to get into a HOE-lot of shit. I didn't care what Sameerah thought; she was coming too.

"Bitch, I'm starving, and I got a taste for some oxtails," I vented. Just the mention of it had my stomach growling.

"At eleven in the morning?" Sameerah quizzed.

"Hell yeah!" We both erupted in laughter. Bahama Breeze was the best spot, so that's where we headed. The restaurant was already starting to get crowded for the lunch rush. Thankfully, we were seated in a booth right away.

Our waiter came and took our drink orders as we looked over the menu. I noticed Sameerah's phone kept going off and she ignored every call.

"Girl, who calls you over there screening?"

"Taizere's ass," she seethed with a roll of her eyes.

"What happened? We got to go beat his ass?" I got hype in my seat.

"I would say yeah, but I know you're serious," she snickered. "I'm just tired of being the only one that's stressing about the bills. Can you believe he took the light bill money to go to the studio? We're going to be sitting in the fucking dark, but at least this invisible ass mixtape will be done." Sameerah shook her head in disgust as our food was brought out.

"So that nigga a bum *and* a thief? You better than me, I would've been left his ass sitting on the curb. I don't even know why you're still dealing with his broke ass. He acts like your damn child instead of yo' man. Have you ever heard any of his music?" I cocked my head to the side.

"Yeah, one song—"

"One song? This nigga be in the studio day and night and got *one* song? You better hope he ain't in there sucking dick."

"Lei!"

"What? Shit." Sameerah rolled her eyes and started picking at her food. "Okay, I'm sorry. I'm just pissed that he keeps putting you in these binds and he's not trying to help. How much do you need for the bill?"

"No Lei, I'll just call and try to get another extension."

"How. Much. Do. You. Need?" I repeated slowly.

"It's eighty dollars," she mumbled. "I swear I'll pay you back."

"Girl shut up." I waved her off. A familiar voice caught my attention, and I turned to see Levi and Micah walking towards us. When Levi noticed us, they walked and slid in the booth with us. Micah sat his ugly ass next to me and my lip raised at him.

"Wassup, sis," Levi nodded at me, then turned to Sameerah, who was looking in her phone. "What y'all up to?"

"Trying to enjoy our food," I added some extra attitude as I cut my eyes to the right of me. "Boy!" I smacked Micah hand down when he tried to grab a piece of chicken off my plate.

"You over here being rude all in your phone while I'm sitting here and shit," Levi said, snatching Sameerah's phone and putting it in his pocket.

"What the hell?" she shrieked. Sameerah reached in his pocket then quickly pulled her hand back like she touched something hot.

"Yeah, that ain't no phone, baby girl." Levi smirked. Sameerah cheeks were visibly red as she put some space between them two.

Looking back and forth between the two, a light bulb went off in my head. I knew Sameerah would leave her mooching ass nigga if she got a real nigga.

3

LEVI

"**Y**ou look like you ain't ever seen a dick before, Lil' Black Girl. I can show you what to do with it," I rapped to Sameerah. Her ass was blushing hard as fuck for me to see the redness in her dark cheeks. I could tell she was a square, so I planned on fucking with her all night.

"Whatever," she grumbled, blushing. "Will you please give me my phone?"

"Say please Daddy Levi."

"Excuse me?"

"Stop fuckin' with her, bruh," Micah chuckled. "She ain't bothering you."

Lei whipped her head and grilled his ass. She scooted over, and that's when I noticed how close they'd been sitting. His arm was draped behind her, and that shit just seemed too comfortable to me. With my tongue pressed against the roof of my mouth, I looked back and forth between the two.

"Don't you think you sitting a little too close, Mic?"

"My fault. I ain't notice," he shrugged and moved away. I looked at Lei and she had her face buried in her plate.

Micah was my best friend. More like my brother, so I

would hate to fuck him up over Lei; if that line was ever crossed. We'd been tight since grade school.

We met when these little niggas tried to jump me for my money. They thought because I wore a school uniform, I would let them bully me. Little did they know, they had me fucked up. I started throwing jabs at all of them, connecting with whoever I could. I slipped, and it went downhill from there. They stomped my ass out, and I was steady talking shit. I couldn't wait until they got tired, so I could get back up and throw hands. Next thing I knew, I heard a few licks being passed and the stomps had let up. I looked up, and Micah was tagging them. I took that as my cue to get up and fight. We beat their asses and took their money. After that, everyone knew not to fuck with us. We became brothers.

Brothers or not, Lei was my blood, and I didn't play when it came to her. Her ass was wild as fuck, but somehow, I kept her in line. Even after being gone for a few years, she knew what was up when I yoked her ass up at the party. The only reason I knew she was there was because I tracked her everywhere she went. Being the man I was, I was protective of her and her wellbeing. Eyes were on her always, and she didn't even know it.

Nodding, I brushed it off and turned my attention to Sameerah. Her little black ass was fine as hell. Square ass. I wouldn't mind giving her the dick, but she was too shy. The shy ones were the crazy ones, and I didn't have time for a bitch to be clingy. That was the quickest way to get you killed. My tolerance for everything is low, so it didn't take much to set me off.

"So, brother," Lei started, and I knew she was about to be on some bullshit. Anytime she wanted something or was up to something, she called me brother. She thought the shit was cute, but I cringed every time she said it.

"Fuck is it now, Lei?"

"You got a boo?"

"Why you askin' dumb shit?"

She shrugged and glanced up at Sameerah.

"Oh, you want me to fuck yo' friend? I will, but her ass wouldn't know what to do with this dick," I called her out, grabbing my semi-hard dick for emphasis. Sameerah glanced down at it and her eyes widened. She blushed and turned away, grilling Lei.

"Leikyn, chill," she warned. "You know I'm with Taizere."

"Taizere is a fuckin' bum ass nigga, Meerah. You know it. My brother a real nigga, and you need to be fuckin' with someone like him. I'm just saying," Lei stated, looking Sameerah in the eyes. "I know you hate hearing how I feel about Taizere, but it's the truth."

"Excuse me," Sameerah mumbled, nudging me with her shoulder.

"Where you going, Lil' Black Girl? Truth hurt?"

"Please... just let me out."

"Sameerah, don't go. I'm sorry, bu-"

"Save it, Lei. I hear you. I'm fine. I need to get home. Now, Levi, will you please let me out?"

"How are you going to get home? You rode with me," Lei pointed out, and Sameerah cursed under her breath. She searched around in her purse, and I smirked. I had a feeling I knew what she was looking for. When she held her hand out towards me, I slapped it and laughed.

"Give me my phone."

"Or what?" I taunted. "The only way you're going to get yo' phone back is if you let me take you home. If not, yo' ass gon' be phoneless."

"It doesn't sound like I have a choice," she groaned.

"You're smarter than I thought. Let's ride. Mic catch a ride from Lei."

"Say less."

I dapped him up and gave Lei the finger. I threw a few bills on the table and led Sameerah out the restaurant. She walked a few steps behind me. I wasn't the type to wait on people, so when I pulled off, she better be inside the car.

I heard her gasp when I hit the locks on my Hellcat. It wasn't my most luxury car, but it was my baby. It was the first car I bought when I got put on in the game. I worked hard as fuck for that car and paid cash for it. Anyone who knew me knew I treated that car like it was my most prized possession. In a way, it was.

She eased her slender frame inside, rubbing her hands against my leather seats. Showing off, I started the engine and pressed the gas a few times. She smiled and fucked up the show when she slammed my door.

"Don't slam my fuckin' door, ma. I don't play about my baby. I'll kick yo' ass out and you'll be walking."

"You're the one who offered me a ride, so please."

"You can get the fuck out. Fuck a nigga for trying to be nice. Matter fact get yo' ass out."

Rolling down the passenger window, I took her phone out my pocket and threw it out the window. She looked at me with her mouth wide open, so I asked if she wanted my dick. Her mouth said no, but her eyes screamed yes. Smirking, I told her to get her ass out and get to stepping.

"No, I refuse. You offered me a ride, so you're going to take me home," she instructed, crossing her arms. "And, you're buying me a new phone. I don't have money for people like you to be breaking my shit. I'm going through enough, as is. Please, don't add to my stress."

"What you goin' through, ma?"

"Don't act like you care, asshole. Can you please take me home?" she huffed, putting her seatbelt on and turning to the side.

I studied her exposed chocolate legs and licked my lips.

She wasn't thick like my usual bitches. She was petite and toned with the perfect amount to grope and feel on. My eyes traveled up to her wet face. *Aw, hell nah.* I had a weak spot for women who cried. I didn't know why, but that shit ate me up seeing a woman releasing her emotions. It was Leikyn and our mama, Lenai's fault. Whenever something was wrong, they cried, and it pissed me off when I could never do anything about it. That's one reason I was so protective of them. Somehow, it turned out I was like that with most women. Not all. Some of the bitches I didn't give a fuck about. They could cry the whole damn Pacific Ocean and I still wouldn't care.

Studying our surroundings, I pulled off in the direction of her house. She didn't say a word as she stared out the window with tears steady flowing down her cheeks. I couldn't help but steal a few glances. I ain't say shit because I ain't feel like cursing her out and hurting her feelings more. Her mouth was too smart for me.

I turned on her street and my phone rang. It was Puffy. He was one of the most loyal workers Mic and I had. He had worked his way up from a corner boy to be the head nigga in charge when Mic or I wasn't around. He had been running shit in The A while we were out in Cali training to officially take over the family operation in all aspects. For years, we controlled the weed and pills coming in and out, but now, we controlled guns, coke, and other things it had been hard to get out hands on. We worked hard to prove to my father, Les, we could take over the family business with no problem.

What most people didn't know was that our father was the head nigga in charge, controlling many states. He kept shit lowkey and covered it up with the many legal businesses he had. For a while, I didn't know until I started catching on to shit. His late-night meetings, security, and other shit made me put it all together. When I turned fourteen, I approached him about it. My father is a real nigga, so he kept it real with me. I was intrigued. Being the preppy, rich, black boy had never appealed to me, and I knew why. Drugs, money, and power ran through my veins, and I wanted to embrace that shit. From that moment, my father put me through training to take over his position. Eleven years later, and I was ready.

Mic's my nigga, so of course, I put him on. My father always stressed how important it was to have a right hand. To have someone by my side I could trust with my life and others around me. Mic was the only other person outside of family I trusted like that. Whatever I had, he did too. I couldn't leave my boy behind.

"What's good, Puffy?"

"You got time to slide by right quick?" he asked, and I knew it was important if he couldn't handle it on his own.

"Be there in ten."

"Bet."

I ended the call and pulled up in front of her house. It was a small, run-down house that needed remodeling. On the side of the house, I noticed the electric company. Sameerah did too because she let out a shrill shriek and hopped out the car.

"Excuse me! Excuse me? Please, don't cut them off! I have the money, but I haven't had a chance to get down to the place to pay it!" she yelled.

"I'm sorry, miss. I can't do anything about it," the man stated, shrugging. He continued working as if Sameerah didn't say a word.

Hopping out the car, I swaggered over to him and shook his ladder. He glared down at me like I was insane, and little did he know, I was.

"Aye, bruh. Take ya' ass on. She said she got the money, so don't cut her shit off."

"I heard what she said," he scoffed, laughing. "It ain't my problem. I'm just doing my job. Next time, she needs to have her money in on time, and she wouldn't be in this predicament."

"My cutoff date isn't for another three days!" Sameerah cried.

My patience for that fat muthafucka on the ladder was thin. Pulling my piece from behind my back, I tapped him on the leg with it. His eyes widened in surprise as I instructed him to climb down. Shaking, he did as I asked and the second his feet touched the ground, I cocked my piece and placed it against his jiggling ass stomach. Sameerah gasped and ran inside.

"Don't make me repeat myself. I would hate to show you the consequences," I warned, pressing the gun deeper into him and smirking. Quickly, he gathered his things and left.

White muthafuckas got me showing my ass in front of this scary ass girl.

Stepping over her threshold, I nodded when I saw the lights were still on. I gave myself a tour of her small crib and went to her kitchen. I settled for a bottled water and fruit before going to find her. She had locked herself in the bathroom, and I could hear her singing. Her voice was angelic and annoying at the same time.

"You need to work on that note, Lil' Black Girl. Shit don't sound too hot," I yelled, taking a sip of my water.

"Why are you still here?"

"Because you need to be thanking me for your lights being on. If it wasn't for me, yo' ass would be sitting in the dark. I'm waitin'."

"Thanks," she mumbled. "You still owe me a phone!"

Laughing, I slid a stack under the door and walked away. Before I could get out the door, I heard her footsteps running up behind me. I turned around and gripped her neck before she could touch me. Not hard, but enough to arouse her.

"Are you crazy?" she screamed, ripping my hand from her neck. She didn't rub it or anything, so her ass was fine.

"Don't run up behind me like that. Shit can get you killed."

"Here," she said, shoving half the money back in my hand. "I don't need all this money for a phone."

"Apparently, you need it for your lights, too."

"Fuck you, Levi. You don't know my story. Just because you're dripping in money doesn't mean everyone else is. Some people still struggle."

"Why you strugglin' if you got a man, Lil' Bl-"

"Sameerah. My name is Sameerah, not Lil' Black Girl."

"You're whatever the fuck I want to call you, Lil' Black Girl. Keep that money, ma. You need it more than me."

I dropped the money on the ground and left her there with her mouth open. I called up Puff and let him know I was on the way. He had called Micah, too. My money better be good, or I was fuckin' some niggas up.

Lighting up some trees, I pulled on it with thoughts of Sameerah. I couldn't front like I ain't want her little ass. She was so innocent, and I wanted to expose her to real. It was apparent her nigga wasn't doing something right, and I had no problem showing her what he wasn't doing. I wasn't on no commitment type shit, but I could see myself fuckin' with shorty.

4

MICAH

"Na if I slap yo' damn head against that wall, you'll swear I was wrong." I grabbed Leikyn by that blonde ass shit in her head and pulled her closer to me.

"You better back up before I bite the shit out of you," her crazy ass snapped at me like she was gon' bite my nose.

"Why you leave like that and not answer yo' phone?"

"Because I'm not competing for no nigga's attention. Since you been entertaining other hoes, you can continue."

"Them hoes don't mean shit. Why you buggin'? When you start worrying about other hoes?"

"Obviously I don't mean shit to you either. Excuse me, I got a hair appointment to get to."

"How the fuck you talkin' 'bout you don't mean shit when I'm going behind my brother's back to fuck with you? Don't I fuckin' take care of you?" Her young ass was starting to piss me off.

"Nigga, I don't need you to take care of me, don't act like you forgot who I am. Now get the fuck out my way," Leikyn snapped.

Before I could go back at her ass, my phone rang, and I answered it. I knew it was gon' piss her off that's why I did it. "Whadup, Puff?"

"Yo I need you to slide on me."

"Bet. On my way." I hung up then slid out the booth and waited for Leikyn to get up. "I need to get to my car."

"That sound personal, nigga." Leikyn was cackling through the parking lot like she said the funniest shit ever. That all came to a halt when I snatched her keys out her hand. "Give me my damn keys!"

"Shit ain't funny no mo', huh? Get in the car." I opened the passenger door and smirked as she threw daggers at me with her eyes.

"I got shit to do for real, Micah," Leikyn complained.

"Aite, where I'm dropping you off at? I'll come back and get you when you done."

"Mica—"

"I ain't got all fuckin' day damn! Where the shop at Lei?" I hit the steering, causing her to jump in her seat.

With squinted eyes, she grabbed my phone and put the address in my GPS. Like the fuckin' brat she is, she sat with her arms folded across her chest and lips poked out. This shit was gon' cost me some money, but she'll get over it.

I had to ignore Leikyn's huffing and puffing all the way to the salon. "Lei Lei—"

"Just drop my car off here when you done," Leikyn interrupted me and got out the car. I'm glad I was driving her shit, so she couldn't slam the door.

Shaking my head, I watched as she switched inside the building. She lucky I had to go because I would've gone in there and made her give me a kiss. I pulled off and headed to see Puff. Crazy enough, me and Levi was pullin' up at the same time. I hope he wasn't about to start with no shit with me about Leikyn's car.

"Why you in my sister shit still?"

"Ay nigga, you been questioning me a lil' too much today."

"About my sister, nigga, I'mma keep questioning' yo' ass. You got some shit to tell me?" Levi approached me with his chest all poked out and shit like he wanted to swing.

"Y'all niggas gon' keep kissing or come in here and handle bidness?" Puff stepped on the porch and got our attention.

"Yo' ass fuckin' trippin' man," I said as I brushed past him and walked in the house. "What's shakin', Puff?" I dapped him up as I walked inside.

"Shit ain't adding up after one of my pickups. I counted the shit five times to make sure I wasn't cappin'," Puff explained.

"Where you get the bag from that was short?" I asked as rubbed the migraine away that I felt forming. I thought when we got the call that we could move back home, that it was gon' be sweet. I planned to be laid up with my shorty, making up for lost time. Not sitting here planning niggas' death.

"Mic, we can ride out tonight," Levi called out.

"Nah, I got this; you go see what Pops wanted." Levi looked at me like he was debating if he wanted to listen before he dapped me up.

"Hit me up when you done handlin' that and watch your back."

"Always."

"Take my sister her shit first," Levi yelled as he made his way out the door.

"That nigga crazy 'bout his sister," Puff laughed.

"Yeah, he ain't the only one. I'm out, good looking out." I dapped Puff up and left. I knew Leikyn was gon' be in there getting her hair done all day so I made some runs before doubling back to get her. The parking lot was full, so I parked right in front of the shop before hopping out.

"Mic, now you know you can't park there," One of these

thirsty broads called out the second I opened the door. Bitches be quick to call yo' name just to make mothafuckas think some shit that it ain't.

"Yeah? Well, my shit parked right there. Where Leikyn at?" I looked around and didn't see her sitting in none of the chairs.

"Her fake bougie ass in the back. You know she can't get her hair done around us poor folk," she snickered.

"Yeah 'cause y'all hoes be in here stealing, I'on blame her. Watch out." I moved her ass out my way and walked to the back. I heard Leikyn loud mouth ass the second I got to the door.

"Yaasss, you slayed this shit as always." I peeked my head in the door to see Leikyn swinging this long ass hair in the mirror. It was blonde and straight down to her ass.

"You getting this long ass weave you probably be sitting on. That shit ain't necessary, ma. Tips of yo' hair probably smelling like shit." I was laughing but stopped quickly when shorty doing Leikyn hair start giggling and shit. If Lei got her ass started up, it was gon' be a fight' 'cause she was gon' swear I was trying to embarrass her or some shit.

"Micah don't get cute in this bitch. I told you to drop my car off anyway. Why are you in here?"

"Aite, Lei." I shot her a warning look and she just rolled her eyes. Leikyn knew how far to go with the disrespect, especially in front of mothafuckas.

"Whatever." Leikyn tried to walk around me, but I grabbed her arm. Without saying anything, I pulled her close to me and kissed them pouty ass lips. "Mmm," Leikyn moaned in my mouth when I squeezed her ass.

"Now we can walk out." I opened the door, and we walked out, hand in hand. I could tell the way Leikyn was staring at me that she wanted the dick.

"You ain't even gotta sit over there daydreaming 'bout it.

Daddy gon' take care of you." It's been a couple months since I been inside my baby and I was about to tear that shit up. After helping Leikyn in the car, I got in and pulled off.

"I know you wasn't eating in my car." Leikyn sniffed around the car until she looked in the back.

"That's yo' food back there. You need to learn to shut the fuck up and go with shit sometimes. Damn." I turned the radio on so I ain't have to hear Leikyn's mouth. It took twenty minutes to get to Leikyn's house with traffic. She still called herself having an attitude, but I know all that shit was gon' change when we got inside.

"What the hell? Micah, you did this shit?" Leikyn laughed as she saw the ten dozen peonies lined up in her living room. I had all the shit I planned to give her last night arranged on the couch for her.

"Damn, why it got to be shit?" I feigned hurt, holding my chest.

"I didn't mean it like that, babe. Thank you." Leikyn batted her eyelashes at me as she wrapped her arms around my neck.

"Daddy did good, huh? So, you done being mad and shit?" I grabbed a handful of her ass and pressed my hard dick against her.

"Let me show you how good you did," Leikyn purred as she unbuckled my pants. Once she had my pants and underwear around my ankles, I gathered her hair in my hand to keep it out her face. This girl is sexy as fuck, and just seeing the way her lips puckered when she popped my dick out her mouth had a lil' precum oozing out. She licked that shit up then smacked my dick against her lips three times.

I was tired of her playing with me and thought about just shoving my dick in her mouth before it exploded. "Aahh fuuuck," I groaned as I finally felt the back of her throat. Leikyn relaxed her throat and took me all the way in her mouth. At this point, I was seeing stars, and little birdies flying around my head.

Pop!

Leikyn popped my dick out her mouth and had the nerve to look up and make eye contact with me. I don't know what type of voodoo shit she doing, but she had the game fucked up.

"Get the fuck up." I snatched her up not caring that she just got her hair done. She just tried to hoe me, and I wasn't goin'. "Hold them legs up and you bet not let 'em down," I warned before diving in between her thighs. It was something about Leikyn's pussy that screamed for me to eat it. It ain't a drug on this earth that give me the same high that her pussy did.

"Ooohh," Leikyn moaned as she guided my head up and down. She dropped her legs down, so I pulled back.

"Hold them legs back up." I snatched her legs up and made her hold them by her ears. I had the perfect view of what I wanted, and I went back to attacking her clit. When I was finally blessed with her nectar, I slurped up every drop until she shook and was pushing my head away.

I snatched Leikyn up from the couch and carried her to the bedroom. The shit I wanted to do to her wasn't about to be limited on that lil' ass couch. "Throw that ass up." I smacked her ass once she was in the perfect arch. After the first stroke, I knew I was about to be in here all night.

"Aahh! Bae, wait!" Leikyn was trying to put her arms behind her to stop me, but I slapped that shit down and grabbed a handful of her hair.

"You wanted this dick, right?" I asked as I pounded into her.

"Uh-Yes!"

"Well shut the fuck up and take it," I growled as I bit down on her shoulder. I slowed my strokes and let Leikyn get in the rhythm to fuck me back. When I felt my nut rising, I made sure I went deep in her guts and let it go. Once I was sure that I got it all out, I pulled out quickly and laid on the bed on my back.

"You want to play games like Plan B isn't a thing." Leikyn started her shit the second she came back from cleaning herself up.

"Shut yo' ass up and come ride my dick." She can talk that shit if she want to but wasn't no Plan B gon' stop my soldiers.

∞

Later that night

I didn't roll my ass out the bed with Leikyn until past one in the morning. I had Puff scoop me and we headed to see these niggas who thought it was okay to be steal from us. When Puff pulled up to the block, it looked like it was a fuckin' party. Music was blasting from the fuckin' trap house, with mothafuckas hanging out everywhere.

"These stupid niggas must've known tonight was their last night," I laughed as I checked my guns. The front door was wide open, so I walked right in and put a bullet in the first nigga I saw.

Pow!

Everybody started scrambling then and reaching for their weapons.

"Turn this shit off!" I screamed over the music. "You bitches got five seconds to get out." The hoes they had in here ran out so fast all I saw was a cloud of dust. It was just four niggas left in the room.

"Mic man, we were working—"

"Did I tell yo' dumb ass to speak? Is that my shit over there?" I used my gun to point to the brick of coke and money sitting on the table in the corner.

"I-I we was gon' pay for it," one the niggas stuttered.

"You was gon' pay for some shit you stole, with some money that you fuckin' stole? Help me figure this out," I asked, walking closer to the group.

"What money?"

Pow! Pow! Pow! Pow!

I hit each of them niggas with headshots before putting my gun up.

"Puff, handle this for me, and make sure you empty them niggas' pocket and package up whatever's left. I'm about to get me a damn Uber home." I was already ordering my ride before I even got done talking. I could've gone to lay up with Lei, but her crib was too far, and a nigga was tired. I'll hit up Levi with what down tomorrow since the problem is already solved.

5

SAMEERAH

"Sss! Suck yo' dick, Meerah," Taizere hissed as I gave him mediocre head. I wasn't putting any effort into it. Lazily, I slurped him. I didn't do all the extra sucking on his head and licking his balls like usual. He didn't deserve the best head I could give. Hell, he didn't deserve it all, but I was tired of him begging.

Picking up my speed, I sucked and jacked him at the same time. He came within seconds. I raced to the bathroom and spit his salty nut down the sink. It left a bad taste in my mouth, so I brushed my teeth. Taizere walked in and glared at me.

"So, suckin' my dick is nasty to you or something?" he scoffed.

"No, Zere. It's early. I haven't brushed my teeth this morning. I need to get to work."

"It's Saturday. Why you workin'?"

"To make extra money. We need it," I explained, washing my face.

Monday through Thursday, I worked at Wells Fargo as a part-time teller. I loved my job and being able to interact with others. It paid well, but not enough. With how things were going, I would need to ask for a full-time position, or get a second job. Lord knows I couldn't handle working two jobs *and* school, but if I had to, I would.

Taizere stood there and watched me get ready. I knew he wanted to say something but didn't know how. I hoped it wasn't anything that would put me in a sour mood. If my day started out bad, then it would be all day. I didn't want that. It was already bad enough I was working on a Saturday because he wanted to be irresponsible.

As I was putting my hair in a low bun, he walked over and pulled my hips into him. He placed soft, delicate kisses on the back of my neck. Closing my eyes, I took a few breaths. He knew that was my spot, but I didn't have time for sex. I had to be at work in an hour.

"Stop, Zere. Let me finish getting ready."

"You not gon' let me feel you before you go to work? It'll make your day better."

"I don't have time, and I can't be late. I gave you head, so you should be good. You got yours."

"Let me give you yours," he pressed, and I could feel his member growing against my ass.

Removing my hands from my hair, he placed them on the sink, palms down. He smirked when he realized I had given in. The sooner we got it over, the better. He wouldn't last but five minutes, if that. It wasn't like I didn't love sex with Taizere because I did, but I held a grudge about the light bill. If Levi didn't drop me off that day, we would have been screwed.

Taizere pulled my panties down to my ankles. I threw them to the side with my feet and spread my legs wider. With his large hands palming my ass cheeks, he placed sloppy kisses between my inner thighs, trailing up to my bare pussy. He sniffed it before darting his stiff tongue deep inside. A raspy breath escaped my parted lips as I held on for the ride. His head game was impeccable. He knew exactly where to lick, suck, or nibble. When I felt his finger insert in my asshole and pussy at the same time, I creamed all over his face.

I leaned over the sink to catch my breath. Taizere wiped his face off and smirked. He rubbed his dick up and down my clit, positioning himself at my slippery hole. I anticipated his thrust, but his phone ringing ruined the moment. Of course, he ran in the room to get it. Groaning in frustration, I washed my private areas and continued getting ready for work. By the time Taizere got off the phone, I was headed out the door.

"Baby, baby, wait!" he called out, catching me by the arm.

"Yes, Zere? I'm going to be late."

"Listen, I need you to run me down to the studio. Trek got some new beats for me, and I need to get there ASAP."

"I'm sorry, but if I do, I'll be late for work. Take an Uber or something."

I masked my annoyance and frustration with a smile. I knew he was trying, so I wanted to take him, but my job was on the line. The saddened expression on his face tugged at my heart. He was so passionate about his music.

"I don't have any money on me," he exhaled.

Digging in my purse, I handed him a fifty-dollar bill. He looked at me bewildered with a furrowed brow. I knew what he was thinking.

"Lei's parents gave me a little money for doing good in school," I explained, lying. Taizere was the jealous type, so if I told him Levi gave me the money, then he would be pissed. I didn't have time to deal with mad Taizere all day.

"Well, I know they gave you more than that. How much did they give you?"

"Why does it matter? It's my money."

"Nah, Meerah," he chuckled, taking a step towards me. I held my composure the best I could, but when he jumped at me, I flinched.

See, Taizere was a little abusive at times. He never hit me, but he would rough me up or purposely leave bruises where no one else could see them. These moments were rare. Still, it didn't change the face I was scared.

"How much did they give you, Sameerah?"

"5... 500," I lied again.

"Give me another fifty. When someone gives you money, it's our money."

Not wanting to argue, I wiped away a tear that disobediently fell from my eyes and grabbed my wallet. I handed him another fifty, and he smiled in satisfaction. Leaning over, he kissed my lips and wished me a good day at work.

"I love you, Sameerah."

"I love you too, Zere."

Looking at the time on my watch, I wanted to cry. I would be at least ten minutes late to work. I was never late, to anything. Oh, well. There wasn't anything I could do about it. I called my manager and informed her I would be late. She didn't act like it was a big deal, so I relaxed some.

I was so stressed and couldn't wait for the semester to come to an end. School and life were taking a toll on me, and I honestly needed a getaway. Usually, Leikyn's parents planned a family trip every summer, and every summer, I declined their offer. I wanted to go, but I needed to work all summer to make more money. I picked up extra hours when I was out for school and tried to save as much as I could. Plus, it was a family trip. I was with Leikyn all year, so I felt she needed time alone with her family. She assured me I was family, and I believed her, but it didn't change my mind.

If they invited me this year, then I would happily accept. I hadn't been out of Atlanta for years, and it was time to breathe new air. Taizere would be in his feelings because I knew they wouldn't extend the invite to him. None of them liked him, and the feeling was mutual. Taizere didn't like anyone I interacted with, and as a result, I distanced myself from certain people. All except Leikyn.

Whipping into a parking spot, I ran inside and clocked in. I got myself together and went to my window to get my day started. Since it was Saturday, the bank was only open a few hours which meant we were busy as hell. The day flew by, and it was time for me to clock out and go home for the day.

"Bestieee!" Leikyn squealed, standing by my raggedy car with a bag of food. I swear she was a lifesaver. I was starving and texted her to bring me some food.

"Thank you so much, Lei!" I snatched the bag and stuffed a few fries in my mouth.

"Come sit in my car. It's hot as fuck out here."

I climbed in her passenger seat and killed my food. I scarfed it down like I hadn't eaten in days. Lei was engrossed in her phone, texting someone fast as hell. I giggled because I knew who it was.

"You and Micah into it?"

"Girl, his ass dumb as fuck. Get on my nerves," she huffed, locking her phone and tossing it in the cup holder. "Did you see your exam results? They're posted."

"Really?"

I logged into my blackboard account and yelled in excitement. I made one of the highest grades on the exam. With the extra credit, I scored a 105 with Lei right behind me with a 103. We studied hard for that particular exam, thanks to me, and it paid off.

"We need to celebrate!" I suggested, thinking of wine.

"Yes, bitch! We need to hit up that party at Basil's crib. You know all his parties be lit."

"Lei, I wasn't even talkin' about *that* type of celebrating. I was thinking more of a girl's night with wine."

"We ain't doin' that borin' ass shit, Meerah! Remember how fun the other night was before Levi's cock-blockin' ass ruined shit? We can redo the turn up tonight!"

Hearing Levi's name sent a shock down my spine. I hadn't been able to get his rude ass off my mind for some reason. Rolling my eyes, I told Lei I would let her know. She demanded I was going and had the audacity to pull off like I didn't drive.

Since she kidnapped me, I agreed. The first place we headed was to the mall, so she could buy a new outfit. Every time she went out, she bought something new. Lei hardly wore anything twice, so I happily took whatever I could fit of hers. I didn't have much, and I was thankful for what she gave me.

"Mom and Pop know you in here runnin' up they limit?" I heard a familiar voice from behind us. His scent grazed my nose, and I knew who it was.

"What's up, Lil' Black Girl?" Levi exclaimed.

"Hey."

"Mommy knows I have the black card, Levi. What yo' ugly ass doin' here? Where's yo' boyfriend, Mic?"

"I'm sure somewhere knee deep in some pussy. I don't clock what the fuck his ass do all the time."

I glanced at Lei, and her entire demeanor changed. She was upset, and I knew she was going to get in Micah's ass later. Levi didn't know but he had spilled the beans on his homie.

We walked in the Gucci store, and Lei went straight to the dresses. Gucci was too expensive for my taste, so I strolled around looking at things I prayed to afford one day. A small clutch caught my eyes, and I couldn't help but pick it up and admire it. I had a thing for clutches, and that one was on my wish list.

I went to put it down, when it was snatched out my hand.

"Fuck you doin' over here by yourself?" Levi asked, licking his lips. He licked his lips so much; I wanted to lick them and see what he tasted like.

"I'm a big girl. I can be by myself."

"Yo', why yo' mouth so fuckin' smart? I just asked you a simple question."

Did he really say my mouth was smart? Every other word he said was a curse word, and he was rude as hell. If my mouth was smart, I didn't know what to call his.

"I wasn't getting smart, Levi. I answered your question."

"Mmhm. You pay yo' light bill?"

"Yes, I did. Thank you, once again."

"Meerah! Come here!" Leikyn called from the dressing room.

Levi followed me over to where Lei had tried on a skin-tight dress. It looked bomb on her body, so I urged her to get it. She urged me to pick something out, but I refused.

"Don't start with that stupid shit, Meerah. You know I got you," Lei sassed, shoving a dress in my hands. "Here, I picked this out for you. I knew you were about to be actin' crazy, so I handled the hard part for you. Now, go try it on."

Snatching it out her hands, she blew me kisses and sat down next to Levi. I tried the dress on, and I loved it. It fit my body like a glove, and the gold shined against my melanin. Lei yelled for me to come out and show her.

Slowly, I walked out, and she gasped. I held my head down because of Levi. I didn't want to look at him. For some reason, I was nervous being dressed like that in front of him. I could feel his eyes scanning my entire body from my freshly, white painted toes to the bun on my head. I glanced up, and our eyes locked. His glare was intense as he nodded his head. Licking his lips, he winked, and I ran back in the dressing room.

"We're goin' to be fine as fuck tonight, boo! Slide the dress under the door, so I can go pay for it."

"Leikyn, are you sure?"

"Shut up, Sameerah. Give me the damn dress."

I put the dress back on the hanger and gave it to her. I finished getting dressed and went to find her waiting for me outside the store, alone. Lowkey, I was butthurt not to see Levi, but also relieved from the way he made me feel.

"Here's your bag. Let's go."

Sitting in the car, I wanted to look at my dress again. I pulled it out the bag, and something else fell out. It was the clutch I was eyeing in there.

"Lei, you didn't have to buy me this," I exclaimed, smiling. "Thank you."

"You're welcome, but I didn't buy it. Levi did," she answered, winking.

"Why?"

"Because, that's how he does things. You can thank him later tonight."

"Tonight? Isn't he too old to be at some college party?" I giggled.

"Yes, but it's been a change in plans. We're hittin' up the club with him and his crew tonight. He asked us to come before he left."

"You know I don't do clubs."

"Well, you're goin' to do one tonight, or I'll have Levi come drag you himself. Don't think he won't."

I wish he would.

I let my silence be my answer. On the inside, I was drowning in excitement. The feeling was wrong, but I wanted to see Levi again. I had to thank him for my things and see him lick those sexy lips again. Maybe going out tonight wouldn't be so bad after all.

6

LEIKYN

"**B**itch, we need to pregame before we get dressed," I sang as I came from behind the bar with a bottle of Crown Royal apple.

"Aw naw, you trying to get some stuff started tonight." Sameerah side-eyed me as I poured us both two shots.

"It's a mothafucking celebration! Pretty soon this school shit is going to be over and the summer is ours." I threw my shots back and poured me two more. I knew I was going to get drunk as fuck tonight, so I set up for a driver to come get me and Sameerah.

"Girl, you gon' be tore up before we even get out the house," she laughed.

"I'm not a rookie like you, I'm good. The driver coming at ten, so you better be ready. I'm about to go take a quick nap." I grabbed the bottle and put it back before going to my room.

The second I closed my bedroom door, I was calling Micah for the hundredth fuckin' time today. It's bad enough he snuck his dumbass out in the middle of the night, then I got bitches popping up in my dm about him, and he got the nerve to not be answering his phone. Then that little slick comment Levi made earlier almost had me going to track that nigga down. This is why I keep telling him I wasn't ready to tell the world about us. Niggas just couldn't get right, but it's cool 'cause I got something for his ass. I know he was going to be with Levi tonight and I was about to show my ass. Knowing he not gon' do nothing with Levi there, it's time I show him who the fuck I am. If I wanted him replaced, he would be, and I'll have another nigga fuckin' me and paying my bills. Not that I needed a nigga to do that, but still.

I had my alarm set for nine to wake me up, and when it went off, I woke up full of petty. I showered and moisturized with the warm vanilla sugar body butter that Micah loved. The dress I was wearing didn't requirement me to wear a bra, so I slipped on some lace boy shorts before doing my makeup.

"Yaasss, bitch. Show that nigga what happens when you ignore Leikyn Symone," I hyped myself up as I twirled in the full-length mirror. I was wearing a rose gold sequin dress that stopped mid-thigh and has a drape neck and backline. I was wearing the strappy heels Micah bought me the other day to bring the outfit together. The only jewelry I was wearing was a choker that matched my dress. Once I doublechecked that I had everything, I went to Sameerah's room.

"Come on let me see your sexy ass!" I yelled as I did a beat on the door.

"You're so extra, I swear." Sameerah opened the door laughing. I eyed my best friend and nodded in approval.

"You sexy as hell, bestie. I already know Levi gon' be behind yo' ass like a thirsty dog," I half-joked.

"I keep telling you I'm not thinkin' about yo' rude ass brother."

"Yeah okay. You can keep telling yourself that lie, I know better. Now come on because I think the driver here." I went to take another shot before going to get in the black Suburban waiting outside. Sameerah had keys to my house so I let her lock up.

Twenty minutes later, we were pulling up to the Compound. I texted Levi when we were pulling up, so he came to meet us out front. When I saw Micah standing next to him, my eyes turned to slits.

"Let's get in and enjoy ourselves a little before you do anything," Sameerah coached when she noticed what I was glaring at.

"I'm good, let's go turn up. Sir, you can stop in front of those two right there." I got out first then Sameerah followed. I could tell the way Levi was eye-fucking her that she'll be occupied for the night and not thinking about the needy child she got at home.

"We got all of upstairs. Don't get in here and act a fuckin' fool," Levi said, looking directly at me. "I don't like that shit you got on," he added.

"Nigga, I'm grown." I waved him off. Even though I didn't want to, I looked at Micah and caught him staring at me. His ass didn't even open his mouth to speak, and he knew better after I sent him those texts cussing him out. Now that I see that his ass is alive and well, I can continue with my attitude.

Ten of us, we moving as one.
I'm so proud of who I've become.
You might think I've taken some lumps.
Only if we talking 'bout sums.

WE WERE TURNING UP TO DRAKE'S SONG TALK UP with Jay-Z. Jay-Z was my favorite rapper, so you know I had my bottle of D'Usse in the air as I rapped along. I was dancing with some random nigga, and Micah was burning a hole in the side of my head. He had his hand on his hip the entire time, and I made it worse by laughing at him.

Fuck boy Mic: You better sit the fuck down before I kill that nigga.

I looked down at the text and laughed again. He was lucky the song went off because I would've stood my ass there and danced some more.

"Can I get yo' number shorty?" The dude whispered in my ear.

"Nah, I'm good. Thanks for the dance though." I smiled as I walked off and took the stairs back to the top floor. I looked around for Sameerah and saw her and Levi caked up the corner. I don't know what the hell he was saying, but I saw all her teeth from here.

"You smell good as fuck. Come talk to me," Micah whispered forcibly in my ear. I looked over my shoulder to see him walking to a booth on the other side of the room.

Reluctantly, I walked to him and sat down. "Now you can talk to me, huh? If you got a problem with me, let me know so I can feel the same way."

"Man, I was handling business today, you know how it is."

"Aw yeah, handling business between some bitches' legs, right?" I crossed my legs and leaned back. My dressed raised a little, but I didn't attempt to fix it.

"I don't know what you talkin' 'bout, me and Levi was together all day," Micah lied so effortlessly.

"That's funny because I didn't see you with him earlier and he didn't know where you were. Save the lies. But you can tell that lil' bitch that messaged me that I'm beating her ass for playing with me."

"What bitch?" Micah scooted closer to me and grabbed me so I couldn't move.

"Whatever bitch that you fuckin' that felt the need to make a fake page to tell me y'all fuckin'. Whatever bullshit you were doing, you should've left it in California. Why come home and do the shit?" I felt myself getting heated and had to calm down.

"You right, I fucked up," Micah admitted. He pushed his dreads out his face and looked at me with those captivating eyes I used to melt for. "I'm sorry, baby."

"Fuck you. I'm not about to go through this rollercoaster shit with you. When you go back to Cali, don't worry about me."

"I ain't going back to Cali, we here for good. So whatever shit you got swirling around in that big ass head, dead it. If you think you about to get on some get back shit with these lame ass niggas, don't. That's my only warning, Lei Lei." Micah was talking so close to my ear that his lips kept brushing against them.

"Well, I guess we're about to have some smoke in the city then, because I ain't fuckin' with yo' friendly ass. Now let me go." I snatched from his grasp and stood from the booth. I walked to where Sameerah was and snatched her up. "Come to the bathroom with me."

"Damn, you just gon' drag me around? Slow down," Sameerah whined.

"I need to get away from Micah before I take a bottle across his head," I ranted as I went in the stall. "He thinks I'm just gon' be one of the hoes he fuckin' and you already know that's not me. Got bitches sending me messages."

"Wait what? What bitches? You didn't tell me nothing about that."

"Because I didn't pay it any mind. But I'm done with Micah ass." I flushed the toilet and washed my hands.

"You saying that now until you're popping up on him to ride his dick again," Sameerah giggled. I looked over at her low eyes and knew she was feeling herself.

"Whatever, heffa. So, if you don't go home and be nasty

with my brother, then you spending a night with me. My parents are having this Sunday dinner and threatened us all about coming."

"Oohh you know I'll be there."

"Come on, I need to find me a new nigga." I checked to make sure my lip gloss was still popping before leaving the bathroom. When we made it to the stairs leading up, I had a bad feeling creep up on me before shots rang out.

Pow! Pow!

"Oh my God, Levi!" I screamed and pushed everyone out my way who was trying to run away from the chaos. When I made it upstairs, I frantically looked around until I spotted my brother. "Levi, are you okay? What happened?"

"Yeah, y'all gotta go, come on." Levi had murder in his eyes as he grabbed me and Sameerah, pulling us towards a door I never noticed before. I looked back and Micah was walking fast behind us. Once we made it to the alley behind the club, Levi let me go. He whispered something in Micah's ear then grabbed Sameerah around her waist.

"I'll text you when I make it in, babe," Sameerah said to me. I rolled my eyes when I realized that meant I was leaving with Micah.

"Come on Lei, it ain't safe out here," Micah smirked as he pushed me towards his car with his hand on my lower back.

"Yeah whatever," I mumbled. "You better be taking me home."

"Yeah, you going to the home I bought for us. Now sit back and shut the fuck up."

I looked at him like he was crazy, but I sat my ass back. Mama ain't raise a fool and I knew when to fight my battle.

7

LEVI

I couldn't believe what the fuck had happened. The first time someone tried to catch me slipping, but they should have known I was too smart for the dumb shit. I peeped it the second they walked in, and I should have handled it then. My attention was elsewhere at the time; still, I knew what the fuck was going on around me. Gritting my teeth together, I knew I needed to murk niggas, ASAP.

Word got around fast. Not too many people knew Mic and I were back in town, so I felt someone close ran their mouth. Sneaky muthafuckas like that were only asking for a death wish that was sure to come. Running my trembling hand over my face, I bit my bent index finger to control the itching I had to pull the trigger on my Glock.

A nigga's hands were shaking so hard; I could hardly control the steering wheel. Blood was the only thing visible in my eyes.

"Levi are you okay?" Sameerah asked, touching my hand. I jerked away, only because her chocolate ass scared me. I was so deep in thought; I had forgot she was in the car.

"My bad. I forgot yo' ass was in the car," I expressed, licking my lips.

"Where are we going?"

"Somewhere."

"You're not going to tell me?"

I didn't reply. My mind was elsewhere, and I needed to focus on that before her. Turning the music up, we cruised in silence until we made it to my spot. I purchased a crib ducked off in Lawrenceville, and the only person who knew about it was Mic. I hadn't even told my folks yet. I wanted to live in peace for a month, so I kept it lowkey.

"Here," I said to Sameerah, handing her my keys. "Go inside and make yourself comfortable. I'll be in there in a second."

"Whose house is this?"

"Who else house it's gon' be, Lil' Black Girl? Dumb ass question, ma. You too smart for that dumb shit."

"Will you come with me? I don't want to go in there alone," she mumbled, gazing at me.

"Scary ass. You a big girl, ma. You're in the presence of a real nigga, ain't shit to be afraid of when you around me. Real shit. Plus, who gon' fuck with some niggas in this white ass neighborhood? Yo' ass fit right in, so gon'."

Cocking her head to the side, she looked at me as if she was unsure. I gave her the same glare back, only with my nose snarled. The tips of her lips curved upwards, but she straightened them before they could fully form into a smile. She exhaled in annoyance and rolled her eyes. Obeying like the good girl I knew she was, she hopped out and slowly walked to the door. I made sure she was inside before calling Puff.

"I'm already on it," he spoke in a low tone. "I got eyes on these niggas now. Need me to save you one?"

See, that was exactly why Puff was the nigga. I hadn't spoken to him, and he was working to handle the problem.

I could hear his right hand, Nash, in the background as well. I informed him to murk all them muthafuckas. There was no need for me to show my face. He agreed and ended the call.

Grateful that I didn't have to leave back out, I sat in the car and burned to get my temper back down. I knew shit would be stressful when Mic and I got back to the A, but I wasn't prepared for anyone trying us so quickly. Not everyone was privy to the fact we had taken over full reign, but they would soon find out. I said there was no reason for me to show my face, but I lied. Putting the half blunt out, I went inside to check on Sameerah. She was sitting on the edge of the couch, looking through an old photo album my mama had given me. It was full of old pictures of Lei and I when we were younger. I took a seat next to her, draping my arm over the couch. Blushing, she scooted over as if she didn't want to be too close.

"Fuck you move away for?" I sneered. She shrugged, so I wrapped my arm around her waist and pulled her closer. "Don't move when I want to be close to you."

"Why are we here? You could have taken me home."

"I didn't want to. Why you so uptight, Sameerah? You're too pretty and shit for all this shyness."

"I don't know you, Levi. So, of course, I'm goin' to be uptight as you call it," she giggled, shaking her head. "You and Lei are so much alike in certain areas. I can already tell."

She flipped through the last few pages of the album and closed it, setting it on the coffee table. Twiddling her fingers, she looked around everywhere but at me. My presence affected her, and I loved it. She wasn't like most females who basically threw themselves on my dick. She showed little to no interest in me, but I knew that wasn't the case. Her lame ass wasn't used to a real nigga like me.

"Aye, check it," I started, squeezing her exposed thigh. "I

DEEANN & AJ DIX

need to run somewhere right quick. You gon' be good while I'm gone?"

"Gone? I'm not staying here by myself! Like I said, you could have taken me home. I didn't ask to come with you. You made me."

"I ain't make you do shit you ain't want to do, Lil' Black Girl. You're your own person. You got a mouth. Speak up and say how you feel. Don't hold shit back for anyone because only you have your best interest at heart, besides me. If you ain't want to be around a nigga, then you wouldn't. Point blank."

"Whatever," she grumbled, not having a comeback. "Will you take me home?"

"Nah, you good. Get comfortable. I'll be back."

Not giving her a chance to respond, I muffed her head and left. Puffy sent me his location, and I sped through the nightly Atlanta traffic to get there. I wanted to get back to Sameerah, so I planned on making it a quick visit. Hitting the button on my steering wheel, I called Mic, and his ass didn't answer. It was cool. I could handle it myself and fill him in tomorrow.

I pulled up to Puff's location and hopped out with my .45 at my side. We were at a ducked off spot I had considered turning into a dungeon for reasons like this. The putrid scent of blood and human waste greeted me before I opened the door. Loud screams and begging echoed off the walls of the empty building, and I smirked in satisfaction. That satisfaction only intensified when I saw Puffy and Nash drilling and sawing two niggas who were unrecognizable.

"Damn, Puff. That's what the fuck I'm talkin' 'bout," I exclaimed, making my presence known. Puff turned around and lifted his blood splattered mask with a blunt hanging from his lips. His ass smoked like a damn chimney, and that's how he developed the name Puffy. He'd been smoking since he was a teenager, and the shit stuck with him.

"Fuck you doin' here, Levi? I told you we had shit under control," he stated, dapping me with his free hand and so did Nash.

"I see, but something was tellin' me to come check shit out."

Nodding, him and Nash stepped back to let me examine the two men. They were hardly breathing, but that didn't stop me from causing more damage and havoc. I strolled over to the tool table and carefully looked over what I would use. The blowtorch caught my attention, giving me an instant hard. The drugs, money, and weed kept me high, but torturing enemies gave me a high like no other. Settling for the blowtorch, I walked back over to them with a sinister grin. One of them opened their eyes the best they could, and when they noticed it was now me hovering over them, they began to cry in fear.

"Le... Levi," he sputtered, blood flying from his lips. "Whe... when you get back?"

"Muthafucka, don't act like you ain't know. Otherwise, you wouldn't have ran up in the fuckin' party," I spat. "Now, tell me who sent you."

"I... I don't kno- aagghhh!"

He couldn't finish the lie before I torched the skin of his arm. I deeply inhaled the aroma of his burning flesh while his sobs sounded like music to my ears. I ran it up and down his arm until he passed out.

"Finish him," I instructed Nash, and went to the next nigga. I slapped him back to life, and he looked around discombobulated. "Speak."

Immediately, he sang like the snitch I knew he was. He informed me that his boss, Rogue, had sent him to take care of us. Word had gotten out about me taking my father's place, and niggas were already coming for my head. Les informed me shit would happen, but I didn't think so soon. I hadn't been back for two weeks, and I was making an example out the two. After receiving all the information I needed, I torched him, too. Just because he wanted to be a snitch didn't mean I would spare his life.

"What's next?" Puff quizzed, throwing lighter fluid over the two dead bodies.

"Keep your eyes and ears open, always. We're already being plotted on, so some changes are comin' ASAP. We'll have a meeting at eight o'clock sharp so get the word out. I'm gone."

Dapping them up, I left them to finish the job. I was tired as hell, but I knew I wouldn't be getting any sleep. My wild thoughts would keep me up all night until the problem was handled.

I made it back to my crib to find Sameerah's ass gone. I searched all over my house looking for her, but she wasn't there. Fuck it. If I wasn't so tired, I would have pulled up at her house. Instead, I opted for a hot shower and some food. Turning on the TV, I watched some Anime while I ate. No one knew about my secret love for it except Lei and my parents. It was my favorite pastime when I found time to relax.

Laying back, I watched until my eyes grew heavy. Closing them, images of Sameerah flooded my brain, and I couldn't help but smirk to myself. Her little black ass had me intrigued, and she was officially on the top of my list. She was mine and didn't even know it yet.

8

MICAH

"**M**icah, you can turn around and take me home because nothing has changed. I'm not fuckin' with you." Leikyn was yapping in my passenger seat as I let the cruise control drive us while I rolled up.

"Hand me that lighter." I sealed the blunt and continued to ignore her ass.

"Get it yourself." Before Leikyn could blink, I was unbuckling her seatbelt and snatching her over to me.

"I'm tired of that disrespectful ass mouth, Lei. You need to remember who the fuck I am." My voice was stern. I didn't even have to get loud. Leikyn was smelling good as fuck and I wanted a taste. I mashed my lips to hers and stuck my tongue in her mouth. When she didn't try to kiss me back, I sucked in her bottom lip before pushing her back in her seat. I grabbed my lighter, lit my blunt, then took control of the wheel.

"You need to stop fucking acting like that."

It took us thirty minutes to get to the house I bought in Lawrenceville. When Levi showed me the crib he bought, I found me one about ten minutes away. Our shit was secluded and that's why I bought it. There weren't any nosey ass neighbors around, and the way shit got wild between me and Lei, that's what we needed.

"Why are we here?" Lei asked when I turned the car off.

"I told you I was bringing you to the house I bought for us." I hopped out and walked around to open her door. Leikyn still had a scowl on her face as she got out and followed me inside.

"Is this supposed to be one of those grand gestures that wins my heart back and I come running in your arms and on your dick? Because I'm not impressed. I don't know why you insist on playing me like I'm one of these weak bitches out here, but you know I'm not that."

"Man speak yo' mind, sitting here speaking in riddles and shit. Fuck is you talkin' 'bout?" This shit was starting to piss me off. Here I thought we could have a nice night of drunken sex, not fighting in the damn foyer.

"This is the shit I'm talkin' 'bout!" Lei shoved her phone in my face it was open to her Instagram direct messenger. It was a picture of me sleeping and this bitch Tasha lying on my chest. I didn't even know this sneaky bitch took the picture. "You creep out the bed with me to go lay up with another bitch? I'm not doing this with you." Leikyn looked me in my eyes, and for the first time, I saw sadness in them.

"Lei Lei, come on, don't do that." I pulled her into my chest and heard light sniffles coming from her. It was fuckin' me up because I never meant to hurt her. Shit, I didn't mean to fall in love with my best friend's little sister either, but shit happens.

It took a minute, but Lei finally stepped back and wiped her eyes. "Show me where the master room is. For the record, you're not sleeping in the same bed as me."

I took her upstairs to the master bedroom, and she walked around examining it. I could tell she was impressed because she kept nodding her head. The house was furnished with the basics, but I had both our closets filled with clothes and shoes. I was leaving the rest up to Leikyn to decorate.

"You might as well grab what you need now because I will be locking this door."

Not wanting to fight anymore tonight, I grabbed some boxer briefs and went to the guest room that was down the hall. When I ran into that bitch Tasha, I was gon' choke the shit out of her for taking them pictures, then sending them to Leikyn. I want to know how the fuck she knew who Leikyn was in the first place, and if anybody else knew.

The next morning, Leikyn was still on her bullshit and acting like she didn't want to be around me. I treated her to breakfast and her ass still wouldn't talk to me. After we ate, I dropped her off at her house because she didn't want to show up with me at her folks' crib.

"I'll see you later, a'ight baby?" I leaned over the armrest to kiss her, and she turned her head, so it went to her cheek.

"See you." Leikyn got out the car and walked up to her door. It opened before she got there, and I was about to hop out and spazz until I saw her little friend Sameerah standing there. My ringing phone got my attention and Tasha's name popped up.

"Heeyy, boo. Am I going to see you today?" Tasha cooed into the phone.

"Yeah. Where you at right now?" I pulled off from in front Lei's house and waited for Tasha to give me directions.

"I'm at home, come on by," she said, and I hung up.

It took twenty minutes to get to her townhome and she had the door unlocked for me. The thought crossed my mind just to kill her ass and go on about my business, but I was going to try the easy way first.

"Hey, I cooked, so I hope you're hungry." Tasha came

strutting her ass from the kitchen half naked, and I had to look away, so I could control myself.

"Nah, I just ate. But what's up with you sending pictures to mothafuckas and shit?" I asked, getting to the point.

"Oh, so I guess I was right. I saw you texting her one day and you were just smiling a little too hard, so I did a little digging. Are you fucking that little ass girl?"

"Bitch, it don't matter who I fuck, you ain't my girl. I think you forgetting that shit up there." I tapped her forehead.

"I know I'm not your girl; you don't have to throw it in my face. But if I'm having sex with someone—"

"That's all it was... sex. It ain't even that no more, I can't fuck with no broad that don't know how to keep their mouth closed. Lose my number, shorty." I coolly walked out and hopped in my ride. I checked my phone, and I had a text from Levi saying Les wanted us at the house early to discuss business. But before that, we had to buss some moves and make sure everything was moving how it was supposed to be.

❧

PULLING UP TO THIS BIG ASS ESTATE LEVI'S FOLKS LIVED IN, I put out the blunt I was smoking. I spotted Levi getting out his whip, so I figured he just got there too. We chopped it up earlier when he filled me in on them niggas they sent home last night. After that dumb shit at the club, we had to switch everything up in case niggas was plotting to hit.

"I'm surprised yo' ass showed up on time," Levi talked shit as he dapped me up.

"Nigga, fuck you, I'm always on time," I countered as we laughed. We walked around the back of the main house and went to one of the guesthouses. This is where Les came to discuss business with us because he wanted to keep business out of his household completely.

"Ahh, it's nice to see you two aren't still stuck on the California time." Les was sitting at the round table with a cigar hanging from his mouth.

"What's good, Pops?" Levi greeted him with a handshake, then I followed.

"I wanted to discuss some things with you two before the girls get here. This year the family trip is going to be different. There's some people that need some convincing that you two can handle the workload that's been given to you."

"Like who?" Levi asked defensively. I looked to him, telling him to chill before shaking my head. I might've been a hothead, but this nigga Levi had a fuse shorter than midget dick.

"Mateo Sánchez, head of the Sánchez Cartel. Also known as the mothafucka responsible for supplying the white girl that feeds them pockets. When you get there, he'll reach out and tell you when and where the meeting will be. Don't get out here and act like you can't hold your shit together. Everything is leaning on this meeting going the right way. Feel me?"

"Yes sir," we chimed at the same time.

"Good, now understand you're going to be traveling with some very precious cargo. I expect you to protect it with your life." Les looked both us in the eye and we nodded. I knew he was talking about Leikyn and probably Sameerah too. Les didn't play about the women in his life and he would kill anybody for even breathing on them wrong.

We sat in the guest house until Mama London was calling saying that Lei and Sameerah arrived. Everybody might've thought Les was this big, scary nigga, but Mama London had this nigga by the balls. I swear if she told him she wants to go to the moon, he'll go buy a damn spaceship. She was a different breed of beast.

"Daddy!" Leikyn squealed as she ran to Les. She jumped in his arms like she was a little ass girl still. That's why her ass is so spoiled, all she had to do was bat her eyes and she'll get whatever she wants, from me included. I didn't even notice I was staring at her until Mama London got my attention.

"Well, hello, Micah, it's nice to see you again." She gave me a knowing look telling me I was busted.

"Hey Ma, you're looking everything young and vibrant today."

"You so full of shit." We both laughed, and my eyes roamed over to Leikyn again. I couldn't help the shit. It was like when she was always near me I had to have eyes on her. "I hope you know what you're doing; those Hart men don't play about the women in their life." Mama London patted my shoulder before turning to call Lei and Sameerah in the kitchen.

"That girl keep playing these games with me, just wait until I get her ass how I want her." Levi was biting his lip as he watched Sameerah walk off.

"This nigga," I laughed and went to the dining area to set the table like we were told to.

Like I said before, Mama London is a different kind of beast.

❧ 9 ❧

LEIKYN

After the night and morning I had, I just wanted to stay home with my wine and watch Netflix. But I knew if I didn't go to my parent's house for this dinner then I was going to hear my mama's mouth for the rest of the year.

Seeing Micah put me back in the funk I was in when he dropped me off earlier. When I got home, I cried on Sameerah's shoulder because my feelings were hurt. I know it sounds crazy since I knew he was probably fucking with bitches in California, but he making these local hoes feel comfortable enough that they'll approach me with some bullshit. I don't even know how the bitch even knew me.

"So how long has this thing between you and Micah been going on?" My mama asked, almost making me drop the pan of macaroni I was holding.

"What are you talking about?" I looked behind us to make sure my dad or Levi was nowhere in sight.

"Calm down, child. I'm not blind; I can tell the way he's staring at you. Then this little attitude you got, I'm guessing something happened." My mama called me out and she was spot on.

"For a few years, but it's complicated, Ma. Please don't say anything because Levi don't know," I whispered.

"Okay, we're going to have to get together and discuss this over lunch tomorrow. And Sameerah, while you over there smirking, I noticed some tension between you and my son, so don't think you're getting off the hook."

"Aaahh haaa," I teased, sticking my tongue out.

"Shut up and go take that food out there." My mama swatted at me and I dodged it.

"I can't stand you," Sameerah mumbled as we walked in the dining room. I couldn't stop laughing.

Once everything was laid out, my mama said grace, and we started to eat. It was quiet at first and all you heard was silverware hitting plates. My mama got down in the kitchen and this food was on point. I was stuffing my face and trying to avoid Micah, who sat next to me.

"So, I'm sure you all know our annual family trip is coming up. But me and London decided to do it differently this year," my dad spoke, breaking the silence in the room.

"What's going to be so different about it?" I asked.

"Well, for one, me and your mother will be going on our own vacation without y'all. Sameerah, I hope you'll be joining us this year, I know Leikyn would go crazy alone." That brought all attention on her, and she looked nervous.

Before she answered, she glanced at Levi then put her head slightly down. "Um, yeah I planned on it."

"Great. We have everything set up for you, so all you have to do is pack your suitcase and go."

"Where are we going?" Not that it mattered, as long as I was far from Atlanta.

"You'll see what the wonderful country of Colombia has in store for you." My mama gave me a goofy smile before cutting her eyes to Micah. My family always loved Micah, so I'm not surprised that she was team Micah. Too bad I'm not messing with his friendly dick ass.

After dinner, my mama made me and Sameerah clean the table and Levi and Micah did the dishes. As much money as my family had, there could've been a whole staff waiting on us hand and foot. My dad claimed it helped build character.

"Huuuh," Sameerah groaned as she tapped away at her phone.

"What your son do now?" I already knew it had to be Taizere's ass.

"Can you take me to my car? He claims he needs it to get to the studio," Sameerah said with a roll of her eyes. I saved my comments to myself because it was only so much I could do.

"Yeah I'm ready, come on." I grabbed my keys, and we went to say bye to my parents before leaving. When we made it to my house, Sameerah hopped in her car and we went our separate ways. Being in the house alone brought me back in my feelings, a place I hated to be.

"OHHH BESTIE, THIS WOULD BE CUTE ON YOU." I HELD UP the cut-out one-piece swimsuit to Sameerah.

"I might as well be naked if I wear that."

"Well, I was trying to keep it a little classy, but if you want to let it hang all out, I'm with it." We laughed.

Ever since my parents told us about the trip, I was itching to go shopping. *Slay Wear* was a new boutique, but they had all the newest fashion. I really only want to buy swimsuits because I planned to be naked the whole trip.

"Uuuhh, best, why is those girls looking over here so hard?" Sameerah whispered in my ear. I turn in the direction she nodded, and sure enough, it was three bitches standing by a rack of clothes staring a hole in my head.

"I don't know, but I smack bitches for fun," I said loud enough for them to hear. They didn't do shit but start giggling to each other.

"Let's just go; it's not even worth it." Sameerah grabbed my arm and pulled me to the counter. I stared at the group bitches trying to see if I knew them from somewhere. Then it clicked.

"Do that look like the same bitch?" I handed Meerah my phone with the dm pulled up.

"Yeah, that's her," Sameerah confirmed what I already knew.

Me: I'm about to drop your bitch in this store. I hope you warned her.

"Ma'am, that'll be $231.60." I swiped my card to pay for the swimsuits. I kept my eyes on them bitches during the whole transaction. My hand was itching to touch one of them.

"I'm so glad you didn't act a fool in there, I'm so proud of you," Sameerah noted as we put our bags in the car.

"Don't be proud yet; I just wanted to get out the store." I sat on the hood of my car waiting for them to come out. Game time. I approached their car and the bitch from the picture just smirked at me.

"I see you got my message," she said with a hint of laughter in her voice.

"Yeah, did you get mine?" Confusion was written on her face. I'm sure the fist that she caught in her mouth answered whatever question she was thinking.

We were in the parking lot exchanging blows. I got the upper hand when she hit the ground, and wasted no time pounding her face in. All hell broke loose when one of her friends tried to grab me.

60

"Aw hell naw!" That was Sameerah. I didn't even have to turn around to know that she was handling business.

Skuuurrtt!

I heard tires screeching and the next thing I know, I was being lifted in the air.

"Who the fuck? Put me down!" I screamed as I struggled to get free. I didn't know who had me or where my best friend was. I just saw black.

"Calm the fuck down," Micah whispered harshly as he pinned me against a truck.

"Yo, we gotta go!" Levi yelled. I followed his voice and saw him dragging Sameerah to his car. Micah did the same as he damn near threw me in my car and hopped in the driver's seat.

"Fuck is you out fighting and shit for?" Micah yelled as he whipped in and out of traffic.

"I told you I was beating that bitch ass when I saw her. She wanted to be funny but know I'm hilarious, nigga." My adrenaline was rushing, and I was ready to rock Micah's ass to sleep next. He looked over at me like he could hear my thoughts.

"Aye calm yo' ass down, if you hit me, I'm hitting yo' ass back," he warned.

"Nigga fuck you. Pull over," I demanded.

"What? I ain't pulling shit over, you not going nowhere."

"I know, nigga you are. Pull over and get the fuck out my car." He must've thought it was a game because he kept driving.

"Lei move!" I grabbed the steering wheel, making the car swerve into the opposite lane. I wasn't playing with this nigga.

"Pull the fuck over!" I swung and connected with his jaw. Finally, he pulled over and hopped out like he was about to beat my ass. I was too quick for him though. I hit the locks and climbed in the driver seat. I sped off as Micah damn near punched a hole in my window. He was yelling something that I couldn't hear.

I saw Levi a few cars behind us, so I knew he was going to pick that dog ass nigga up from the side of the road.

Meerah: Bitch, you fucking crazy! This nigga is going to kill you!

I laughed at the text and kept driving home. If Micah pulled up on bullshit, then I was gon' have to shoot his ass. He better be lucky I don't make him get my nails fixed.

❧ 10 ❧

SAMEERAH

"What the fuck is yo' sister problem, bruh? You see what her crazy ass did?!" Mic shouted in anger. His long dreads were flying everywhere as he threw his hands up in the air. I watched in the mirror as he laid down in the backseat and threw his forearm over his eyes. "Y'all family got some fuckin' issues, Levi. I swear y'all need to get checked out."

"Fuck you, Mic. Fuck you do to my sister? She wouldn't throw you out for no reason," Levi exclaimed, and I had to agree. Knowing their dilemma, I knew it was because of those girls at the mall. I wasn't the type to fight, but I would never let anyone jump Leikyn. I rode for her like she rode for me. I was reserved, but I wasn't a punk.

"I didn't do shit but snap back at her retarded ass! She fuckin' spazzin' for no reason. I swear her ass needs to be on some meds or something."

"Watch yo'self, nigga. I'll put yo' ugly ass out too if you keep talkin' stupid. Use yo' damn legs."

"Fuck you."

I couldn't help but giggle at them. They sounded like an

old married couple. Their bond was solid like Leikyn and mine. I loved it. My smile vanished as I thought about how it would break once Levi found out about Lei and Micah. I'd always told Lei it would come to light one day. She knew it too but wasn't ready to accept it. That was understandable. I just hoped she prepared for it mentally and emotionally. Seeing how crazy Levi was over her, things would get really ugly.

"Why you in the corner thinkin' shit so comical? Why yo' lil' chocolate ass out here bein' ratchet with Lei? That shit ain't cute, Sameerah," Levi snapped at me. I inhaled deeply and looked out the window. I couldn't handle the side-eye he gave me.

"What was that shit about anyways?" he asked.

"Ask Micah," I mumbled under my breath. Levi didn't hear me, but Micah damn sure did. He kicked the seat so hard I jerked forward. I peered back at him and if looks could kill; well, you know.

"Call and ask yo' sister, nigga. I'm sure Sameerah ain't have shit to do with it. She was probably dragged into some of Leikyn's shit."

Screaming, I covered my head as Levi slammed on his brakes. Car horns blared, and tires screeched loudly. I anticipated the crash I was sure to come, but never did. Levi rolled his window down and cussed everyone out who passed by talking mess. Micah was right; their family had issues.

I was thankful we weren't on a busy road because Levi threw the car in park and turned to face Micah. His jaw clenched as he mugged him. Micah sat up and returned his glare.

"Problem, nigga?" Micah questioned Levi.

"What's yo' problem with my sister? You speakin' on her with loose lips, Mic."

"Fuck you gon' do about it, Levi? I ain't pussy. You can get it if you want it. One of y'all need y'all ass beat."

"Sayless."

The doors flew open, and I could only think of one word to describe how I felt: scared. Two grown ass niggas got out the car to fight, and I mean they were fighting like they weren't best friends. I didn't know what to do, so I sat there and watched. Micah won in my opinion, but I wouldn't tell them that.

Once they got back in the car, Levi drove like a madman. They were both breathing hard and I could feel the anger radiating off them. I hoped Lei and I never fought like that. I could hold my own, but I wouldn't want to be on the other side of Lei's wrath. She was too crazy for me. Apparently, Levi was too.

We pulled up to Micah's house, and I nodded in approval. Lei told me how nice it was, but I didn't expect it to be so nice. His house made my little home look like a shack. It was close to Levi's house, so I was surprised it was beautiful.

"I'll get up with you later," Levi said, dapping Micah up.

I looked at them Levi in confusion as he backed out the driveway. Since his face was towards me, I could see a cut right above his eyebrow. Micah must have hit him hard. He glanced at me and frowned.

"Fuck you all in my face for? Like what you see, Lil' Black Girl?"

"You're bleeding."

"And? A little blood ain't ever hurt."

"Why are you so rude?" I griped, sitting back and crossing my arms.

"If you don't like what comes out my mouth, don't say shit to me. I'm rude because I'm Levi."

"I see."

"Aye, where you take yo' ass to the other day? You dipped on my ass. I ought to drop yo' ass off like Lei did Mic."

"I went home. I told you I didn't want to be there by myself. You told me to speak up, and I did. Don't be surprised by my actions."

"Keep listenin' to daddy," he chuckled, winking at me.

Why was he so fine? That wink damn near made me melt in the seat. I turned my head, so he wouldn't see me blushing. I had to stay away from him, but it was hard. Levi was like a magnet, always pulling me in even when I didn't want him to. It was as if he was everywhere I was or something. Weird, but I couldn't explain it.

I hid the disappointment I felt when he pulled up in front of my house. For some reason, I knew he would take me to his. I got my hopes up, so I couldn't be upset with anyone but myself.

"Be ready at eight," Levi demanded when I grabbed the door handle. I looked back at him, and he mugged me. "You heard me, Lil' Black Girl. Don't make me repeat myself."

"Wh-"

My car pulling into my driveway stopped me from completing my sentence. It was Taizere. I honestly didn't expect him to be home during the day, so he'd caught me off guard. Fear took over as I thought about how jealous he was. Taizere didn't like me around other men or even talking to them. I knew he would flip when he saw me in the car with Levi, alone.

"Is that yo' nigga?" Levi asked, pointing to Taizere, who had gotten out the car. He started towards the car, and my heart dropped. I prayed it didn't end how I knew it would.

"Yes. That's my boyfriend. Thanks for the ride home."

I opened the door, and Levi said, "Remember what I said. Be ready at eight."

Quickly, I nodded and shut the door. Taizere mugged me

but didn't say anything. That wasn't a good sign. His silence always meant an ass-whopping was soon to come. I wanted to turn around and get back in the car with Levi. I could feel his eyes burning a hole through my back. If I turned around, it would only make things worse.

Taizere pulled me into him, looking in Levi's direction and placing a kiss on my lips. I cringed when he discreetly bit my bottom lip. His bite was hard and long, bringing tears to my eyes. He pulled away and pecked my lips before slightly pushing me towards the house.

Once I was inside, I tried to get away from Taizere fast, but failed. Before I could get two steps away from him, he caught me by my hair and yanked me back. I yelped out in pain, but it didn't stop him from pulling.

"Who the fuck was that nigga, Meerah? You out here fuckin' around on me?" he growled in my ear. I felt his hand go up the back of my shirt and whimpered when I felt his hard pinches against my skin. Taizere was a different type of abusive. Still, it didn't take away the fact that he was an abuser.

"Ouch, Zere! Stop, please!"

"Who the fuck was he?"

"Le… Leikyn's brother, Levi. Lei… ouch! Lei got into some trouble at the mall, and he had to bring me home," I explained in between tears. "Please, stop!"

Letting my hair go, he spun me around and shoved me against the wall. He studied my face. All I wanted to do was break down and cry. I hated when he got in his little moods and tortured me. He was such a different person when he got like that.

"Why you in the car with that nigga alone? Why the fuck I smell him on you?"

"I just told you, Zere. I'm telling the truth, I promise."

"Whatever, man," he smacked his teeth and walked away.

I stood against the wall until I felt it was safe to move again. I wanted to avoid Taizere, so I went to the kitchen to fix me a sandwich. My back was sore, and I knew it would be bruised and irritated. It wasn't the first time he'd done it.

Sitting at the table, I ate my sandwich and scrolled through my phone. Curiosity got the best of me, and I looked Levi up on social media. He didn't have anything. I wasn't surprised because he seemed like the lowkey type. We had that in common, unlike his wild sister.

I jumped when I heard Taizere grab my keys and leave, slamming the door behind him. He didn't say one word to me, so I figured he was going to the studio. The time on the microwave read it was a little after five. He wouldn't be back until after midnight, especially since he was pissed at me. I was perfectly fine with it, only because I wanted Levi to come back and get me.

It was wrong, but I was excited. The thought of being around him more made the hairs on my body stand. He was so different from Taizere, and I believed that was one reason I was so intrigued by him. They were both rude as hell, but Levi's came from a good place. I could tell. As for Taizere, he was like that because he knew I wouldn't retaliate. I wasn't the argumentative type, so he picked when he felt like it. Knowing how he was, I would never hear the end of Levi bringing me home. Him being Leikyn's brother would only make things worse.

To pass by time, I decided to get ahead and study. Finals weren't for another for weeks, but I wanted to ace all of them. It would require tons of studying. In between working and trying to live, I would get no sleep.

I couldn't wait for the trip to Colombia. I'd never been out of the country, so I was super excited. A trip was something I desperately needed. Taizere would be pissed, but he would get over it. I refused to not take a free trip because of him. He was one of the reasons I needed a vacation. I loved him, but he was like taking care of a child.

By seven o'clock, I was in the shower. I wanted to take my time doing my make-up and hair. All Levi said was that he was picking me up, so I had no clue where we were going. Keeping it simple, I put on gray shorts with a teal top and the sneakers to match. I straightened the curls out my hair and applied a natural beat to my face. Looking in my mirror, I smiled in satisfaction and snapped a quick picture. I hardly ever posted any pictures I took, but I loved taking them.

My phone rang, and I expected it to be Levi. Instead, it was a number I didn't recognize. I was skeptical about numbers I didn't know, so I never answered. When they called for a third time, I gave in and answered.

"Hello?"

"Mee Mee? It's yo' mama, baby."

11

LEVI

"What's good, boo? I'm glad you stopped by," LaLa cooed.

She was a broad I used to fuck around with before I went to Cali. She was cool as fuck and would suck the skin off my dick anytime I demanded. LaLa was nasty as fuck. That was the only reason I'd agreed to stop by her crib. I hadn't had any pussy since I got back in Atlanta, and a nigga was in need. LaLa was thick as fuck, but like some Atlanta broads, she had ass injections. Her shit looked natural, though. It damn sure jiggled like it was.

"You know I'm only here for yo' mouth."

"Damn, it's like that?"

"Ain't it always been? Don't start actin' like shit is different," I hissed, mugging her dumb ass. If she was about to be on some clingy shit, then it was cool. I wanted no parts.

"I was just sayin', Levi. I thought you would at least ask how I'm doin' or something. It's been so long, an-"

"You gon' shut the fuck up and suck my dick or what? If not, I'm about to bounce, La. I got shit to do."

70

Rolling her eyes, she kissed her teeth and spat, "I should have known you didn't change."

"You damn skippy, La. So, like I said," I paused, dropped my gym shorts and boxers. "Suck that shit hard."

I smirked when LaLa dropped to her knees and crawled over to me. Wrapping her small, cold hand around my dick, she nastily swirled her tongue around my head before taking me in, inch by inch. I let her have control, enjoying how she fucked me with her mouth. Leaning my head back and closing my eyes, I grabbed the back of her head and thrusted deep in her mouth until she gagged. Her eyes watered, and her hands hit my thighs in a plea for me to stop. The fear in her orbs sent me over the edge, and I nutted deep in her throat. I pulled back as she fell to the ground, choking on my kids.

"I notice everything, La. I'm very aware of my surroundings, even with my dick down yo' throat. Give me my fuckin' wallet, bitch."

La had given me some of the best head I'd ever had, but I felt when that sneaky bitch traveled her hands down my legs and into my shorts. I wasn't stupid, if that's what she thought. La had never tried any shit like that, but I wasn't surprised she did. The only thing she accomplished by using her grimy fingers was signing her death certificate. She knew the consequences like everyone else. Just because she was a female didn't mean I would show any mercy on her ass.

"Wha... wha..." she couldn't finish the lie on the top of her tongue. Her eyes darted left towards the door like she planned to escape. Snickering to myself, I pulled my shorts up, never removing my eyes from her. LaLa tried to take that as her opportunity to escape, but she wasn't fast enough. She got up and ran for the door, but I tripped her causing her to stumble back down. She tried again, so I stomped on her back and held her down with my foot. Retrieving my gun from my body holster, I cocked it and shoved it into the back of her nappy ass head.

"Levi, I'm so-"

"Shut up, bitch."

I sent a bullet straight through her skull, basking in the way her head almost exploded. I called clean-up, double checked to make sure I didn't leave anything and dipped. Looking at the time on my phone, I saw it was a little after seven. I stopped by my parents' house to shit and shower since they were closer, before going to scoop up Sameerah. I didn't have any plans for us, but I would do whatever she wanted. I wanted to chill and get to know her better outside of Leikyn. Last time I tried, her little black ass hauled ass, but I'd be damned if she tried it again. I wouldn't hesitate to hold her hostage. She didn't know it yet, but she was mine. Fuck that nigga she claimed. From the way Lei spoke about him, he wasn't any good. Thinking of that reminded me to get some information on him. I didn't like the vibe I got from him earlier.

When I arrived at my parents' crib, I went to my room and straight to my closet. I settled for some khaki shorts and a plain black tee. For the most part, I dressed simple. I didn't get flashy until I felt it was needed. My presence alone spoke volumes, so there was no need for it constantly. I laid it out on my bed, emptied my pockets, and went to the bathroom. I was showered and dressed in ten minutes. As I was coming down the steps, Ma was coming up them.

"Son, what are you doing here? I didn't hear you come in," she explained, hugging me and kissing my cheek.

"That's not good, Ma. Pops and I've told you about bein' aware of your surroundings."

"Boy, I got this."

"Umph. Where's Pops?"

"Out having a drink and cigars with his friends. You got time to sit and chat with your mother?"

"You know I always have time for my favorite woman," I answered, smiling. Ma and I had always had a close relationship. The older I got, the closer we got. Like Lei, I was protective of her; probably more than anyone. If anything ever happened to her, I would lose my shit. The little I had left.

"Where are you headed to?" she pried with a raised brow. "You sure smell good."

"I always do. Why you bein' so nosey?" I teased, dodging her swing. She didn't play, and she was who Leikyn got her attitude from. Damn Sour Patch Kids. "Nah, I'm about to go chill with a Lil' Black Girl."

"Sameerah?"

"How you figure?"

"Boy, you know nothing gets by yo' mama. I saw the way y'all looked at each other. It was cute. Sameerah is a good girl, Levi. Poor child can't take anymore. Between her egg donor and that no-good boyfriend of hers, they're already doin' enough damage," she griped, rolling her eyes. "She needs to get away from him. He's not on her level and never will be. She doesn't need to stoop down to his. She needs a man who matches her."

"You're lookin' right at him. It's cool, Ma. Watch how I change her life." I was deadass about it, too. I had claimed Sameerah as mine. She just didn't know it yet.

I kicked it with Ma until eight. I figured Sameerah was like most females, especially her best friend, and was never ready on time. To my surprise, her little chocolate ass was waiting on the porch for me. Immediately, I could tell something was off about her. She wasn't smiling and shit like normal, so I studied her movements carefully. She was timid like she was in pain or something. The grimace on her face when she sat back made my nostrils flare. Her face was screwed up in a mixture of pain and frustration.

"Hello to you too, Lil' Black Girl," I started. "You just get in folks' cars and don't greet them? That's rude as fuck."

"Sorry. Hey, Levi," she grumbled.

"What the fuck is yo' problem? If you gon' have an attitude, you can get the fuck out."

"FINE!"

Sameerah threw her hands up in the air and got out, slamming the door behind her. I'd told her little ass about that shit. Hopping out behind her, I jogged to catch up to her.

I grabbed her by the shoulders and spun her around. Her smooth, mocha skin was covered in black tears. I kissed my teeth because that wasn't the shit I felt like dealing with. She jerked away from me and stormed inside. The soft part deep within me caused me to follow her.

Once I was inside, I shut and locked the door behind me. I went to find Sameerah. She was laid out across, what I assumed was her bed, crying her eyes out. Running my cupped hand over my face, I sat next to her and picked her up, placing her in my lap. She buried her face in my neck and sobbed.

"Why you cryin', Sameerah?"

"As if you care."

"I wouldn't have asked if I didn't. I wouldn't be sittin' here holdin' yo' lil' ass if I didn't. Trust, you would know if I didn't care. My car wouldn't be outside right now."

"Why does so much fucked up shit keep happenin' to me? I try to be a good person and do right by the universe, but I always get shitted on in return."

"I'm gon' keep it one hundred; the universe doesn't owe you a gotdamn thing. The quicker you learn that; the easier shit will get. You can't expect to always get what you give. It's fucked up, but it is what it is."

"What's the point, then?"

"Point of what?"

"Living. If it's goin' to be like this, then I rather not be here."

"Whoa, Lil' Black Girl. I'm about to take yo' ass to the mental hospital if you're suicidal. I ain't built to deal with that shit. I'll give you a gun and tell you to go for it."

"Wow," she giggled, sitting up and wiping her tears. "Some help you would be if I was."

"Oh, well," I shrugged. "You gon' tell me why you're cryin', though?"

"Do you really want to know?"

"Fuck it."

I pushed her off my lap and walked towards the door. Her ass was going to learn I only asked questions because I wanted to know the answers. If she wanted to keep asking dumb questions, she could talk to her damn self. I was almost out the door when I felt her small, soft hand grab my elbow. By reflex, my hand went around her throat, again. That was something else she needed to learn. I didn't like people sneaking up behind me.

"Sorry," she gasped, taking a step back as I released my grip. "Don't go, please."

"You gon' stop askin' dumb shit?"

"How are my questions dumb?"

"See," I chuckled. "There you go again."

"Whatever. Will you please stay? I need someone to talk to, and I know Leikyn gets tired of hearin' me ramble about my pathetic life."

Sameerah led me to her worn out couch, and it was the first time I got a good look around. I could tell she'd tried to make it look like something, so I gave her props on that. She worked with what she had, but she deserved better.

First, she started with her bum ass nigga and how he was

an upcoming rapper. I didn't know what she thought upcoming meant, but that nigga wasn't it. How the fuck was he rising with one song and never been heard of before? I listened as she vented about how she was the only one paying the bills and working. Basically, that muthafucka used her. That was how I saw it. I understood why my mama and Lei didn't like him.

"You got a bum ass nigga, Sameerah. He ain't shit."

"He's tryin'."

"Bullshit. You dumb as fuck if you think that, but that's yo' business. Stay stupid and watch where you get. Nowhere."

"Tell me how you really feel," she griped, rolling her eyes.

"I always will. You need a real nigga, Sameerah. A nigga that's gon' take care of you and shit. You're too smart to be so dumb. I've been stressin' that shit to you since I met you. Keep fuckin' with me. I'll make you forget about yo' nigga."

"You already do," she admitted in a whisper. She looked down at her exposed thighs then back at me. Licking my lips, my eyes roamed her body.

"I know. You ain't ever fucked with a nigga like me."

She blushed and scooted closer to me. Laying her head on my shoulder, she exhaled heavily. Next, she told me about her mother.

How she'd been taking care of her and herself all her life since her mother was an addict. The waterworks started again, and I didn't say shit. After hearing her story, I knew why she was so dumb and naïve. She never had anyone to teach her shit. I was surprised she'd made it so far in life.

"She called earlier, saying she was clean and wanted me to come see her. I don't believe her, Levi. It's the same cycle. She'll be clean for two weeks and fall right back in the trap the second I hand her some money."

"Stop givin' her money, Sameerah. That'll solve that shit."

"It's easier said than done."

"Nah, it really ain't. Don't hesitate to cut muthafuckas off who mean you no good, including family. If you know it's the same cycle, why continue it? You got the power to break that shit, baby girl."

She looked off in the distance and nodded. I could see she was in deep thought, and I hoped she took in what I said.

"Thanks for listenin', Levi. I feel a lot better."

"I can be a gentleman when I want to."

Before she could say anything else, I gripped her chin and parted her sweet, pink lips with my tongue. At first, she didn't kiss back, so I deepened the kiss. Our tongues danced inside each other's mouths, and my dick was hard as fuck. Her little black ass was skilled with her mouth, taking my mind elsewhere. When she moaned, I pulled back. I wasn't trying to have her dickmatized, especially with the headspace she was in. I pecked her lips once more and smirked.

"Let's go get some food before I fuck yo' little ass on this couch."

She nodded and scurried to the back to get her shoes. Yeah, she was mine and whoever had a problem with could get that work.

12

MICAH

It's been a few days since Leikyn lost her damn mind and I was letting her calm down before I tried to holla at her again. When she hit me in my shit when I was in her car, I was ready to beat her head in. I was happy as hell when Levi started with his shit so I could take my anger out on him.

Now, I'm missing my baby and she ignorin' the fuck out me. I called her ass all night until she put me on the block list. I knew she had class today, so I was sitting outside her school waiting for her to come out. When I saw her walking out with Sameerah, I ashed my blunt and stood by her ride.

"I'm about to go get my ass back in bed. You need to let me know if you coming to get yo' hair done when I go." Leikyn was running her mouth and looking in her phone so she didn't see me.

"Uh, best," Sameerah said, giggling. She was trying to warn Leikyn, but her bighead ass wouldn't look up. When she finally did, she rolled her eyes and stuck her phone in her purse.

"What do you want, Micah?" This girl was really actin'

like I was getting on her damn nerves or something. I had to keep telling myself I fucked up, so I couldn't yoke her ass up.

"I want you to holla' at me, Lei Lei."

"Nah, I'm good." Leikyn tried to move around me, but I grabbed her arm.

"Umm, I'm going to go, bestie. Call me later. Nice seeing you again, Micah." Sameerah waved then pranced her ass to her lil' beater.

"Leikyn, stop fuckin' playing so much, you being real disrespectful," I said into her ear as I had her hemmed against the car door.

"Oh, like yo' disrespectful ass, right? Let me go before you not be able to have kids," Leikyn threatened, looking me in the eye.

"If you put yo' hands or any part of yo' body on me that's not in a sexual way, I will happily take whatever Les do to me after I beat yo' ass." I pulled her around to my car and put her in the passenger seat. I laughed when I saw she tried the door, but I already had the child lock on.

"I'm not leaving my car out here; this is kidnapping, Micah!" I ignored her and pulled out from the parking lot. "I have plans, I don't have time to play with you right now."

"I heard you say you getting back in the bed, so we can get in that mothafucka together. Now sit back and shut up." I turned the music up and hopped on the expressway.

I parked in the garage and let it down before I got out and opened Leikyn's door. "What happened to your lip?" Leikyn pointed at my mouth.

"Your brother, shorty. I had to beat his ass since I couldn't get to you," I half-joked. I did beat his ass though.

"Aw yeah," Leikyn shrugged like it wasn't shit.

"Come on and lay down so I can rub on your booty and talk to you."

"Nigga, you can talk to me without touching my ass. I

79

already said what I had to say though, bro; I'm not messing with you." I laughed and followed behind her to the room.

"The fact that you really believe this is funny as hell. You ain't going nowhere this shit for life baby girl. Just wait until you have my baby, our daughter gon' be pretty as hell."

"Micah, if you think I would ever have any of your big head ass babies, you got me messed up." I grabbed a handful of her hair and pushed her against the wall.

"I wish you would think you getting rid of my baby. I'll slap you and whatever doctor helped you do that shit. Stop saying dumb shit before you piss me off, take them outside clothes off, mane." I stepped out my basketball shorts and got in the bed.

"You better be lucky that I'm tired," Leikyn mumbled and took off her clothes. She took one of my t-shirts from my drawer and put it on.

"I'm sorry for hurting you, Lei, you know I love the fuck out of you. I deleted all them hoes out my phone; we can start over."

"Micah, I just really need time to think about all that. You know my mama know something? I been avoiding her since that dinner because I know she's going to tell my daddy."

"Good, I'm too grown to be sneaking around and lying and shit."

"You not sneaking around because I'm not messing with you," she repeated like that meant something.

"Sshh, I'm trying to sleep and shit." I closed my eyes, but I could feel her staring at me.

Finally, she laid her ass down, and I pulled her close to me. Leikyn could talk all that tough shit, but I could tell by the way she snuggled under my chin that she missed me like I missed her.

I didn't realize how tired I was until I woke up and it was dark outside. I didn't feel Leikyn next to me, so I jumped up and turned the lights on. I still saw her purse and clothes. I breathed a sigh of sigh knowing she was still there. I didn't even realize how much of a bitch I was for Leikyn until now. I was fucking sick when she was ignoring me, she even changed her locks, so I couldn't get it.

"What you standing there looking lost for?" Leikyn came out the bathroom wrapped in a towel.

"Shit I am lost. What time is it? Where my phone at?" I looked in the pockets of the shorts I had and found my phone. "Damn," I said, looking at the time that read 9:37pm.

"I'm hungry." Leikyn folded her arms across the chest and stared at me. I had to stop myself from going over there and snatching that towel off her ass.

"What you trying to eat man? You know we got a cabinet and fridge full of groceries."

"That's gon' take too damn long, I want some barbecue, so you need to hurry up before they close."

"How you gon' get fresh then rush me," I mumbled, grabbing some sweats. Leikyn eyed me for a second then went back to getting dressed. "Where you trying to go, or you want me to pick?" I asked once we were dressed and in the car.

"It doesn't matter." Leikyn shrugged and grabbed her phone. Just like that her attitude was turned back on, and she was being short with me.

I took us to a small barbecue spot that I found last week and parked. Knowing Leikyn, she was wondering how I knew about this place and thinking some bitch told me about it.

We walked in the restaurant and I nodded to the owner, who was standing by the door.

"Ooohh, I want some of everything." Leikyn fat ass was drooling as she looked at the menu.

"Get whatever you want, bae." I pulled her to me and placed a kiss on her forehead when it was our turn to order. Hell yeah, I was laying it on thick right now.

We decided to dine in and sat at a booth that was by the window. Leikyn was acting like she didn't want to look at me as we waited for our food to be brought out.

"Come on, Lei Lei; you can't be that mad at me over that shit." I broke the silence.

"Why wouldn't I be? How would you feel if a nigga I was fuckin' with while you were gone decided to message you?"

"I would kill any nigga you called yourself fuckin' with, so that's not an option. Ain't no real nigga sending no other nigga a message anyway," I laughed.

"That's your fuckin' problem, you think shit a joke all the time, well I'm not playing with yo' ass. You had me out here actin' like a damn hood rat and I don't like that shit."

"I know, bae and I'm sorry. We can start over and move as slow as you want. If you don't want to tell yo peoples yet, that's cool." The server brought our food out, interrupting our talk.

"Micah, you know I been loving you damn near all my life and I feel like you took advantage of that. I'm focused more on me now; if you can't respect that, then I don't know what to tell you."

"How long is that shit supposed to last?"

"As long as I say it is, Micah, you not controlling this situation this time," Leikyn said with finality. "And you're taking me home when we leave here."

I just nodded and ate my food I couldn't argue with her stubborn ass. I see I got to win her heart back and all that other lovey shit. Leikyn can play this game if she wants to but ain't no way she was moving on with no other nigga but me.

After Leikyn got her banana pudding, I paid the tab, and we left. I took her home like she wanted and waited until she was inside before pulling off. I drove over to the trap to check on money since I was out. We had to make some examples outta niggas too, so they know what type of time we were on.

But they still wouldn't stop a nigga from trying you. If I had to kill the whole team and start over, then I would.

I pulled up to the rundown house we had downtown not far from the campus, and I could smell the money moving in and out that mothafucka. Being by the college was like a guaranteed bag every night, especially with the amount of parties that went on over here.

"What's going on, Mic, you here to collect already?" One of the lil' niggas asked when I approached the property.

"Nah, I'm just making sure niggas on they job, but I see it's all smooth over here." I eyed my surroundings, making sure shit wasn't out of place.

"We good, might need a reup soon."

"A'ight, you know what to do when that time come." I nodded and walked back to my ride. Ain't no point in me being out here with these lil' niggas if I didn't have to be. All I had to do was go my ass back home and figure out how to get my lady back.

13

SAMEERAH

Since Levi and I kissed, I'd been trying to avoid him, but he made it hard. It was as if he was everywhere I was. School. My house. Leikyn's. We'd grown closer, and I was getting to know him. He was so different, but in a good way. Levi was hard. Unlike Taizere, who used abuse as his dominance, Levi was rude, but sweet. He didn't care what he said to anyone, whether it hurt their feelings or not. I was sensitive, so his words got to me often, but I was learning not to pay his tone any mind and listen to what he said.

Taizere noticed my distance, so he'd been on his best behavior. He was still in the studio heavy, but he came home at a decent hour and had been the nicest person. I knew he felt bad for bruising my back. He wouldn't admit it or apologize for it, but I knew him. He was trying to make up for it by his actions.

I loved Taizere because we'd been through a lot together. I believed in him and his rap career, but since I'd been around Levi, those feelings were slowly beginning to diminish. Well, I can't say slowly; more like rapidly.

I was annoyed by Taizere's presence. I wanted him to be

out all night, so I could have more time to myself and with Levi. It was so calm and peaceful when he was gone. When he came home, all Taizere talked about was his rap career. I listened because I cared about his career, but it wasn't the only thing we had to talk about. Every now and then, he would ask me about school and work. Even then, he would cut me off and somehow direct the conversation back on him. After a while, I gave him short answers because I knew he didn't care. Levi did. He showed interest in anything I talked about. His listened without interrupting, except when he had a smart comment to make. I could compare the two all day, and I knew it wasn't good.

Before my date with Taizere later, Leikyn and I were going to get a little studying in. I needed to talk to her about my feelings for Levi, but with all she was going through with Micah, I didn't want to drown her with my problems. I honestly didn't want to go on a date with Taizere, but he wouldn't stop begging. I much rather spend time with Levi.

I hopped in my old, faithful car, throwing my backpack to my passenger seat. Taizere caught an Uber to the studio earlier, which I paid for. It was better than him asking to use my car and me being without transportation all day. I tried cranking my car, but it stalled. It took three times before she cranked up.

As I drove, I thought about my mother. She'd been calling begging to see me. She promised she was clean, and it would stay that way. Deep down, I knew she was.

I could hear the difference in her voice and it made me happy. I didn't want to have full faith in her, though. I didn't want to get my hopes up that it could be the time for her. Like any other addict, only she could determine when she would stay clean for good. Anytime I thought I would give in, Levi's voice played in my head. I wanted to see my mother since I hadn't in months, but I knew I would become weak once I laid eyes on her. She would butter me up, ask me for money, then run off once I gave it to her. I wouldn't hear from her for months, maybe a year. I couldn't keep going through that cycle with her. It was unhealthy for the both of us.

The more I thought of how my mother chose drugs over me, her one and only child, I became disgusted with her. I felt I was doing so well in life without her, and it pained me to realize it. All the positive steps I'd taken in life, I'd taken without her. It was every girls' dream to have their mother by their side, rooting them on and giving them advice on how to continue moving in the right direction. She was supposed to be my shoulder to lean and cry on when I made the wrong decisions. I had to learn everything on my own. Once Mama London came into the picture, I had the guidance I needed. I truly appreciated her. Still, I wanted it to be my own, blood mother.

"What's going on?" I groaned as my car putted out smoke and slowly came to a stop. Hitting the stirring wheel, I put on my emergency lights and got out to check what was going on. I wished I could have got to the median because cars were flying past me, and I was scared. Just as I was about to give up, a nice SUV parked behind me and threw their caution lights on. A handsome, tall man hopped out, jogging over to me.

"You need any help?" he asked, face dripping with concern.

"Yes, please. I have no clue what I'm doing. It started smoking and just stopped."

"I'm pretty handy with cars. Let me take a look."

I stepped back and let him do his thing. I texted Lei to let her know what happened, so she wouldn't fuss about me being late. She texted back saying Levi was on his way, and I got a little happy inside. I figured I wouldn't see him today, but somehow, fate always allowed me to.

The man looked at my car for fifteen minutes until he closed the hood and shook his head. He informed me what I already knew; my car was gone. I was so upset. I loved my little car, especially since I had brought it with my own, hard-earned money. I thanked him and offered to pay him something. He was a complete stranger who went out his way to help me.

"I would never take money from you, beautiful. But, I would take your number, if you wouldn't mind," he flirted, and I blushed. I couldn't believe he was hitting on me. I opened my mouth to speak but was cut off by Levi's rude self.

"Nah, she good, bruh. Only number she need is mine. Ain't that right, Lil' Black Girl?" he interrupted, winking. "'Preciate the help. You can go, homie."

All I could do was shake my head. The man looked as if he wanted to protest until Levi lifted his shirt, showing off his gun. I hated he carried it everywhere.

"I don't mind using it, especially when it comes to her," Levi threatened.

Nodding, the man excused himself and drove away. Levi looked me up and down before instructing me to get in the car. First, I retrieved all my things from inside my car. He waited by it until a tow truck got there to take it away. I couldn't help but shed a few tears watching it being taken away. That car had given me a few good years. Now, I had to think of how to get a new one. The money I had saved was for a house, but it looked like I would have to spend some of it on transportation. It seemed as if I always took three steps forward and ten back. Something had to give.

Levi hopped in the car and headed to Lei's house. I sat with my arms folded, looking out the window. I could feel Levi glaring at the back of my head. Turning to him, his expression was blank. I couldn't figure out what he was thinking.

"What's wrong?" I asked after seconds of awkward staring.

"Were you goin' to give that nigga yo' number?"

"Huh?"

"Huh?" he mocked me. "Don't play stupid, Sameerah. You heard me."

"No, I wasn't."

"That's what I thought."

I rolled my eyes and smiled at his smart ass. He reached over and grabbed my hand, kissing the back of it. It was a sweet gesture, one he'd never did before. I was beginning to think Levi was getting soft on me.

We made it to Lei's house. I asked Levi if he was going to stay, but he said he had business to handle. He kissed me bye before I got out and went inside the house. Lei was sitting in the middle of her floor with books sprawled out everywhere. None of them were open, and she was deep in her phone.

"Doesn't look like you're studying to me," I teased, slapping her phone out her hand. She swatted at me, picking her phone back up.

"I'm tryin' to make sure Mic stupid ass isn't actin' out on social media since I told him I was doin' me."

"Why you say that to him? We both know Mic has you wrapped around his finger."

"Shut up, Meerah," she spat. "He doesn't have me wrapped around his finger. I just love his ass, too damn much. I'm tryin' to pull back from him and his damn shenanigans. I can't allow him to have control anymore. I was faithful to a nigga who couldn't give me the same fuckin' courtesy. I feel like he played and took advantage of me, and I ain't with that."

"I understand what you're saying. I think the two of you

need to come clean to everyone about y'all. Mama London knows, so I feel everyone else needs to. Y'all are grown."

"I know, but it's not that easy. I don't want to talk about it anymore," she mumbled.

I let it go because I didn't want her in her feelings. I knew what she meant about it not being that easy. Once Levi and Les found out, I wasn't sure her or Micah would be breathing after they got done with them.

We studied for hours to prepare for finals. They were a few weeks away, so I wanted to prepare as much as possible. We'd already applied for graduation and were waiting on our caps and gowns. I couldn't believe the time was almost here. The time for us to step out into the world and pursue what we loved. I planned on applying for a promotion at the bank I worked at. If I could secure a higher position, it would help tremendously.

"So, what you doin' tonight? Spendin' time with my brother?" Lei pried as I stuffed my books in my backpack.

"I wish," I mumbled to myself. "No, Taizere and I are going on a date?"

"Why?"

"What do you mean why, Lei? He's still my boyfriend."

"I knew my hoeish ways would rub off on you, but I didn't think it would include my brother. You know how I am about Levi, and you know how he is about me. We don't mind letting people know what it is with our hands. I love you, and you're my girl, but stop playin' with my brother, Sameerah."

"I'm not tryin' to," I huffed, offended. I couldn't believe she would assume I would be that type of person.

"Yes, you are, and you're playin' yourself. It's evident y'all have feelings for each other, and you're no longer interested in Taizere. You need to end things with him if you're goin' to continue entertainin' my brother. I'm tellin' you this because I love the both of you. Figure it out, boo."

Nodding, I could understand where she was coming from. Like she said, her and Levi were protective of one another and only wanted what was best for each other. I knew I had to decide, but it wouldn't be easy. Leikyn wouldn't understand. I didn't think anyone would. I loved Taizere, but I wasn't in love with him anymore. I wanted Levi, but I couldn't just drop Taizere to be with him. It wouldn't be fair to him.

"Do you mind taking me home?" I asked when I remembered what happened to my car. I got sad all over again.

"So, how are you and bum ass going on a date with no transportation?"

"Shit. I didn't think about it. I guess we'll have an inside date. There's something in the fridge and cabinets I can whip together."

"If you say so. I should take you to my brother's instead of home."

"Whatever."

We rode in a comfortable silence to my house. Lei had her own shit to think about, so I welcomed her quietness. I knew she was thinking about Micah, and honestly, I hoped they could work it out. They loved each other, and I felt they deserved to love one another openly without judgment. Too bad the world didn't work that way.

When she dropped me off, I noticed Taizere peeking through the blinds. Lei told me to call her if I needed anything and drove off when I made it inside. Taizere stood there waiting, fully dressed.

"Where's your car? Why did she drop you off?"

"My car broke down in the middle of the road, Zere. It's dead, so I have to buy a new one when I can."

"When did that happen? Why didn't you call me?" he pried through gritted teeth.

"I called Leikyn since I was closer to her and because she

could have come to get me." Once those words left my lips, I silently cursed myself. Taizere cocked his head to the side and squinted at me.

"Who came to get you if she didn't?"

"I had an Uber take me to her," I lied. "She had just gotten out the shower, so I told her I would catch a ride there."

He folded his arms and studied me. I studied him back, thinking of what Lei said. The man who stood in front of me wasn't the same man I'd fallen in love with years ago. Or, maybe he was, and I was no longer blind to it. The thought of ending things with him crossed my mind, but I wasn't brave enough to do it. Not yet, anyways.

"A'ight, baby. What you gon' cook, then?"

I breathed a sigh of relief. I didn't want him interrogating me about my life. Thinking, I went and sat my stuff down and raided the kitchen to find something to cook. To my surprise, Taizere helped. Of course, he talked about himself the entire time, but it was something different.

You need to decide, Sameerah. You can't keep this up.

14

LEIKYN

The best thing about the end of a semester is having the professor give us the option to come in or not. The only thing they were concerned about was making sure we passed finals, which I knew I was. So instead of going to class, me and Sameerah was on our way to go to lunch with my mama. I avoided her as much as I could, but she popped up on my doorstep and made me get dressed. I wasn't in the mood to talk about Micah while I was trying to forget him.

"Soooo," my mama started, breaking the awkward silence we were in.

"So what, Ma? You the one that dragged us out here," I smartly replied. The look she shot me to let me know not to play with her today.

"Okay, lil' girl, yo' daddy not here to save you today," she warned with an eye roll. "Since you want to be funny, I'm starting with you. When did you and Micah start being grown? And before you lie, I know you doing something with all that sexiness around."

"Ma, please." I shrunk down in my seat and held the menu over my face.

"I'm just saying, if I was a few years younger—"

"I'm about to call my daddy," I threatened. Sameerah was laughing hard until I shot her a look. She threw her hands up in surrender but was still giggling behind her menu.

"Ain't nobody scared of Les." My mom waved me off. "Now talk."

Sighing, I said, "It's been like four years, but we not on that level no more." I shrugged nonchalantly.

"Why? You couldn't get your way with something?" My mama accused.

"No, because he got a friendly dick and I'm not about to be out here embarrassing myself just to say I got a man." I was getting madder the more I thought about it.

"I'm not saying you need to forgive him, but you know that boy is crazy about you, hell I can tell that by the way he looks at you. Did you give him the okay to mess around?"

"Ma, do I look like one of them dumb broads? When he was in Cali with Levi, we had a clear understanding that he was gon' do him and I was gon' do me, he just decided to keep the mess going out here too."

"Mmmm. Well, it seems like he gave you what you was asking for. You don't ever be happy with half a man; I taught you better than that. Yo' daddy tried that shit and got a cast iron skillet to the back of his head."

"Ma, you supposed to be on my side."

"I am on your side, baby, that's why I have to tell you where you messed up at. If a man really wants you and only you, a little distance not going to change that. Now, Ms. Sameerah, on to you." My mama turned her chair halfway towards Sameerah and I was glad that she took the heat off me. Since I'm sitting here in my feelings, Sameerah was about to be too.

"Yes, ma'am?" Sameerah tried to put that sweet voice on.

"Don't yes ma'am me, lil' girl. When did you and my son start tangoing?"

"Wh—? We're not doing that," Sameerah stuttered. Her face was flushed, and it was my turn to laugh at her.

I sat back listening to Sameerah lie about just being friends with Levi until the waitress came to take our order. After I told her what I wanted, I excused myself to the bathroom. I had that weird feeling like I was about to come on my period and I needed to put a panty liner on. Thankfully the bathroom was empty, and I went in the stall.

"What the hell?" This is day fuckin' ten, and my period still haven't come. I was a person who is never later, and I mean never! I start panicking thinking about the possibility of being pregnant. What am I going to do with a baby right now? I'm still living my best life, and I haven't even started on my career yet.

I heard the bathroom door opening, so I hurriedly wiped myself and got up. I saw Sameerah standing in the mirror pretending to fix her hair and I laughed. "You in here hiding from my mama?" I asked as I washed my hands.

"It's not funny, Lei," Meerah whined.

"I'm glad you came in here though, I need you to go somewhere with me after this." I grabbed a paper towel and Sameerah looked at me funny.

"Lei, if we about to go beat somebody ass, I need a change of shoes."

"Girl shut up. I'm not about to do all that," I laughed. We went back to the table as our food was being brought out.

As we ate our food, my mama talked about graduation and the trip. I'm glad we leave the day after graduation to kick off our celebration. My mama paid for lunch and we went our separate ways.

"So, where we going?" Sameerah asked the second we got in the car.

"You'll see, girl damn. What you trying to go run off with my brother?"

"Shut up, and for your information, yes, and I told Taizere I was staying with you tonight; in case he asks."

"First of all, that nigga know not to ask me shit. And second of all, oohh you spending the night?" I smirked at her as she rolled her eyes.

"Mind yo' business." Sameerah turned the radio up to drown out my laughs.

We pulled up to Walgreens ten minutes later and I hopped out before she could ask questions. I quietly strolled through the store to the aisle with the pregnancy tests. I heard Sameerah gasp.

"Are you serious? I'm about to be a God Mommy?" Sameerah beamed.

"I don't know that's why I'm here. Can you get one of them helpful hoes to come open this up?" She walked away skipping and shit.

She came back with a guy and I was mad that he was cute. "Thank you," I mumbled and snatched a few different boxes down and went straight to check out.

I blocked out all Sameerah blabbing about baby showers, baby names as I drove home. I'm glad I didn't see Levi's car parked outside. He always seemed to pop up when he knew I was going to be with Meerah.

Before I went to the bathroom, I grabbed a bottle of Smart Water out the fridge. This weirdo brought a stool in the bathroom and sat at the door. There were still a few feet between us but damn.

I had to drink the whole bottle of water at once before I got the urge to pee again. There was a little cup I peed in and I dipped each of the tests in there; I had four in total. I wiped, then placed the test on the sink. I washed my hands and stared down at the test the whole time.

"Lei, staring at them is not going to make it pop up faster. I already know you pregnant, you b een sleeping a lot and eating weird shit."

"Well bitch, why you ain't tell me?" I don't know why I yelled at her like she had something to do with it, but she should've warned me or something.

"Mmm, look at them raging hormones, it's probably a boy."

"Bi—" I was cut off by the sign of an alarm on Sameerah's phone and both of our eyes went down to the tests. All of the tests were positive and I felt my stomach drop to the floor.

"Damn, I was joking, but you really pregnant." Sameerah's face mirrored mine. I threw the test in the garbage and washed my hands again. I walked in my closet and start going through the stuff with tags still on it.

"Help me find something cute to wear, I got a date tonight," I told her.

"With Micah? Are you going to tell him?"

"No, my boo Nathan. Are you about to help me or not?" I stopped to look at her.

"You gon' get that boy killed, but I think you should wear this." Sameerah shook her head and handed me a nude colored, bandeau hem, bodycon dress I ordered from Pretty-LittleThing.

"Thanks, boo." I ignored her comment and took the dress.

"Well, Levi is on his way, so I'll see you later. Call me if you need me." she hugged me and went downstairs. She had keys, so I knew she was going to lock the door.

I started the shower and put my bonnet on and when the water was hot enough, I stepped in.

At first, I just let the water run down on me, my hands

went to my stomach, and I couldn't believe this nigga got me. It's not like we used protection so ain't no telling when this happened.

My daddy is going to kill me.

∞

"I'M GLAD YOU FINALLY TOOK ME UP ON MY OFFER," Nathan said from across the table. I met him a few months ago when I was getting my car serviced, but it never went past us texting or talking on the phone.

"Me too, this place is nice," I admired the dimly lit restaurant we were in.

"It's a new spot, but I heard they food was pretty decent." The waiter came to take our order.

My phone vibrated on the table and I quickly grabbed it to silence it. I knew it was Micah because his ass had been calling me all day every day. I was a second from changing my number.

Mic: You need to come talk to me.

I rolled my eyes at the text before responding.

Me: I'm busy leave me alone, Mic. I told you I'm done with that shit.

Mic: If I come in that restaurant, it's gon' get ugly.

My eyes bucked, and I looked towards the door. I didn't see anyone at first, but sure enough, Micah's Range Rover was parked in front of the restaurant, and he was standing in front of it.

"Everything okay?" Nathan got my attention.

"Yeah, sorry about that." I smiled nervously and put my phone in my clutch. I felt my phone vibrate again, but I ignored it.

DEEANN & AJ DIX

"I see you think I was playing," I heard behind me, and the hairs on my arm stood up. "Stand up," Micah said as he snatched me from my seat. He shocked me when he sat down and pulled me in his lap.

"Let me go." I tried to pry his hands from my waist, but I couldn't.

"What's your intentions with my bitch?" Micah asked Nathan, further embarrassing me.

"Look, bro, I don't know what's going on, but I'm not trying to step on nobody's toes." The way Nathan bitched up turned me all the way off.

"Nigga what?" I asked Nathan, voice laced with attitude. When I met Nathan, I told him I had a man, and he was talking all that tough shit like he wasn't worried.

"This the type of nigga you want, Lei Lei? Let's go, Ma, you better than that." Micah was enjoying this too much. He tapped me on my thigh, so I could stand up, and handed me my clutch off the table.

I didn't even bother looking at Nathan or saying anything as I walked out the restaurant with Micah trailing behind me. He opened the passenger door for me and helped me in. Surprisingly, the drive back to his house was quiet.

Micah pulled into the garage and we walked in through the kitchen. Before I could make it to the stairs, Micah grabbed me and pulled me into him, and sniffed the back of my neck.

"You really got all sexy and shit for another nigga?" Micah's voice was rough as he whispered in my ear. My words were stuck because I was getting horny. "Answer me."

"Yeah," I whispered.

"You wanted to give my pussy to that lame ass nigga, Lei?" He grabbed a handful of my hair and started placing kisses on my exposed neck. "I'm so sorry, baby; I'll keep saying it until you forgive me. Whatever you want me to do, I'll do it." I felt

98

something wet hit my shoulder and tried to turn around, but he had a grip on me.

"Mic—" I started to say, but he interrupted me.

"Tell me you forgive me, Lei baby," he pleaded.

"I forgive you," I finally admitted. Finally, he loosened his grip and I was able to turn around. I got emotional seeing the tears on his face. I wiped them for him and stared his eyes.

I thought this would be a good time to tell him about me being pregnant, but when he leaned down to kiss me, I got distracted and happily accepted his lips. I'll tell him when the time is right.

15

LEVI

I arrived at Lei's house, and Sameerah was sitting on the porch waiting for me. A smirked turned the corners of my lips as her chocolate face lit up when she noticed my car.

She stood up, straightening the sundress she had on. It was dark green with gold studs outlining the V-neck. It was different, but Sameerah made anything look good. Her hair was in a ponytail, giving a better view of her gorgeous facial features. Her little sexy ass. She knew what she was doing.

Her sweet, fruity perfume greeted me before she did. Before she could close the door, I leaned over, gripped her face, and kissed her glossy lips. Eagerly, she kissed me back. I had missed the feel of her lips.

"You look good, Lil' Black Girl. I see you dressed up for daddy," I noted, winking.

"I felt like looking pretty today. That's all."

"Say what you want. I know what it really is. I like that shit, too. Keep it up and watch what I do to you."

I peeled from the curb and headed to my crib. Like always, I asked Sameerah about her day. I loved hearing her tell me what went on in her world. She would apologize for talking so much, but it didn't bother me. It was obvious she wasn't used to it.

In the middle of her talking, my phone started ringing and stopped abruptly. Holding my finger up for Sameerah to pause, I pulled it out and silently cursed under my breath. It was my father. When he called like that, it meant he wanted me wherever he was in less than an hour. Seconds later, a text came through informing me he was at home. I wondered what it was about. I was close to their house, but Sameerah was with me. It would be cool. My mama would keep her company.

"We need to go to my parents' house for a second," I informed her, pressing the gas harder. I called Micah, and he said he was headed to their house. If Pops called both of us, it had to be important.

I glanced over at Sameerah, and she looked uncomfortable. She squirmed in her seat, rubbing her hands together.

"What's yo' problem?"

"Nothing."

"Speak yo' mind. It ain't that hard."

"What do you think your parents are going to say when they see me walking in with you?" she spoke, peering at me with wide eyes.

"I don't know, and I don't give a fuck. We're both grown as fuck, Lil' Black Girl. They can't say shit about what we do."

"I know, but... I have a boyfriend. They know that. I don't want them lookin' at me differently."

"So, that's what it's about? You don't want to look bad?" She nodded. "Like I just said, you're grown. Everybody knows you're fuckin' a fuckboy, so they'll be happy to see you with a real man like me. Don't stress."

"It's still wrong."

"Why you here if you feel like that? We're just friends,

Sameerah. I ain't gon' lie, I got feelings for you, but at the end of the day, you're another nigga's woman. I vibe with you and I like your company, so I'm always gon' try to be around you when I can. I'm tryin' to make you mine, but I ain't tryin' to rush you, either," I rapped to her. I was game to her shit. Sameerah wanted to keep her 'good girl' image, and I understood that, but everyone had a little bad in them.

"I want... I like you too, Levi. It's different with you, but... I feel..."

"You feel like you owe yo' nigga something? Let me be the first to tell you; you don't owe him a damn thing, or me. The only person you owe something to is yourself. Once you realize that, you'll be a lot happier."

I turned my music up to end the conversation. It fucked with me knowing she felt the way she did. I didn't feel bad for entertaining and pursuing her because I knew she would be mine. Being the man I was, I wanted to let her figure it out on her own and decide what she wanted in life. She needed to put herself first to be happy. If Sameerah kept her mom and Taizere first, toxic people in her life, she would never learn.

Our ride was silent until we pulled up to my parents' house. Mic waited for me in his car and jumped out when I did. He dapped me up and smirked at Sameerah as we walked inside. I told Sameerah to go find my mama while Mic and I headed to my pop's office.

"You know what he wants?" Mic asked, and I side-eyed his ass.

"Does it look like I know?" I griped, knocking on Pops' door.

"Enter," he bellowed out.

Opening the door, I saw my father sitting at the desk with a strained expression. He ordered for us to sit at the seats in front of him. He continued looking over something without speaking. When I couldn't take the silence any longer, I leaned over and snatched the paper from under him. Usually, he would get in my ass about something like that, but he remained quiet as I observed what had him stressed.

"Mateo on some fuck shit?" I quizzed, passing the paper to Mic.

"Not Mateo, but one of the other suppliers that works for him. They know I've passed shit down to the two of you. They think since you're young, you can't handle it. Mateo sent that to me earlier. Apparently, Buck wants to take over all my territories. Mateo wasn't with it, and I have a feeling Buck will try something funny. He'll be in Colombia when y'all go, so I need y'all to be the men I know y'all are and handle him," Pops explained, leaning forward with his hands clasped together. He looked back and forth between Mic and me.

"You already know we'll handle it, Les. We ain't about to let anyone bitch us," Mic spoke.

"Especially not a pussy nigga from Alabama," I cosigned.

On the inside, I was heated. I hated when people under-estimated me and what I was capable of because I was young. My age didn't have shit to do with how I conducted business, and I planned on showing Buck and whoever else how I rolled.

"Be smart, son," Pops stated, chuckling. "The two of you are both hot-headed. I need you to go into this with a clear mind and a plan. Don't go in there thinkin' you can just kill him, and that'll be the end of it. Just like any other man, he has an army behind him that will go to war. Since you will have the girls with you, I'm sending your best men to accompany you on the trip. Strategize and be smart. Don't fail or I will pull you down and hand it over to someone else. Understood?"

"Don't play me, Pops. You know what I'm about. This will be smooth sailing," I assured him, smirking. His smirk matched mine because he knew what it was. I had his blood running through my veins.

"So, what happens after we end that nigga's life? Do we take over his territory?" Mic asked, rubbing his hands together.

"Of course. It'll all be yours. Mateo knows how shit works, so he won't be a problem. It's just how the game works."

"We got you," Mic expressed.

Pops went over a few more things with us before dismissing us. Mic left while I went to find Sameerah. She was in my mom's sitting room, talking and giggling. I sat back and watched the two interact. From the glow in Sameerah's eyes, I could tell she adored my mama. It was hard not too when my mama was the shit. I knew it stemmed down to her own mother not being there.

"Y'all in here talkin' about me?" I interrupted, sitting next to Sameerah. I gripped her thigh and squeezed it.

"Son, no one is worried about you," Ma giggled. "We're havin' girl talk, that's all."

"Mmhmm. Girl talk means y'all talkin' about niggas."

"Not always," Sameerah said. "Our world doesn't revolve around men."

"Tell him, baby."

"See, y'all ain't about to double team me. Bring yo' ass on, Sameerah, before I leave you here with my mama hatin' ass."

"Watch yo' mouth, Levi! Just because you're tryin' to show out in front of Sameerah doesn't mean I won't pop you in your mouth for cussin' around me," Ma snapped with a deep scowl. Sameerah giggled uncontrollably like it was the funniest thing she'd heard.

"Whatever, man. Come on, Sameerah. Love you, Ma."

"Love y'all, too. Remember what we talked about the

other day, Levi. It was nice seein' you, Meerah. Come keep me company more often."

"Yes, ma'am."

I let Sameerah walk ahead of me to the car. My mind was on what Pops laid on Mic and me. Shit was lowkey stressful already. My plans were to go to Colombia, handle business with Mateo, and enjoy my time with Sameerah. Now, it'd turned into a fuckin' war; one I didn't want Lei or Sameerah around. I texted Mic and the crew to let them know we needed to meet soon to get the plan together. I didn't know who we were up against, but my pops did. I texted him, too, letting him know I would need his presence at the meeting. He would be our personal inside man to kill that Buck muthafucka and take all his shit. I wanted things to go smooth and quick. We just had to map shit out precisely.

"Do you have other female friends, Levi?" Sameerah said out the blue. I smirked at how bold she was to ask that.

"What you think, Lil' Black Girl? I'm a single man. Of course, I got other female friends," I kept it real.

"Oh."

"Oh, what?"

"I don't know."

"You jealous? You want daddy all to yo'self," I teased. A smile tugged at her lips as she folded her arms across her bosom. My eyes trained on the plumpness of her breasts. With one hand on the steering wheel, I reached over pulled her arms down. Before she could fold them again, I had one of her breasts filling my hand. She gasped but didn't stop me from pinching her erect nipples. Sameerah's teeth clenched together as I massaged her breasts. Not once did she try to stop me. Her little ass knew what it was.

"I bet you wet as fuck right now. Open up and let me see."

"Levi, I can't."

"What's stoppin' you? Nothing. I'm hard as fuck, so I

know you got a puddle under you. I bet yo' nigga don't make you feel like that." Her face tinted red and she looked out the window.

I decided to quit fuckin' with her until we made it to my crib. Throwing my car in park, I killed the engine and got out to open her door, but she was out before I could. I led her inside, locking up and setting the alarm.

"I love your house. I'd love to live somewhere like this one day."

"You could have better than this if you were fuckin' with me on that level. Why you insist on takin' care of a bum ass nigga?"

"He's no-"

"Ain't no lyin' in my house, Lil' Black Girl. You can get yo' ass out if you about to take up for that nigga."

She sighed heavily, rolling her eyes. She tried to walk off, but I caught her by the back of her arm. I pulled her body into mine and slid my hand under her dress. Sameerah's body tensed up, but she never moved. She laid her forehead against my chest as my fingers found her pussy. Like I knew she would be, she was soaking wet. My fingers almost drowned in her wetness. I thumbed her clit while working two of my fingers in and out her tight opening.

With my free hand, I lifted her face from her chin and parted her lips with my tongue. The longer we kissed, the harder I grew. Her pussy juices made sloshing sounds as I finger fucked her. My kisses went from her lips to her neck. Inhaling her sweet scent, I got high off the intoxicating smell before attacking her neck like a vampire.

"Oh, Leviiii," she moaned, grinding her hips against my fingers.

When she did that, I said fuck it and replaced my fingers with my dick. I knew I shouldn't have gone inside her raw, but it felt good as fuck. Sameerah's pussy swallowed my dick.

The suction mixed with how wet she was made me want to nut prematurely. I had to slow my pace and think of something other than how good her pussy was.

Her legs were looped in the creases of my arms and her ass was barely on the counter. It was the perfect position for me to hit her spot repeatedly. Her nails clawed my back and her sexy moans filled the house. We ended up fuckin' all over the house for hours. Her little chocolate ass had stamina. She let out all her feelings on my dick, and I didn't mind one bit.

We laid up in the bed after our last round. We had showered and ate, talking about shit. Shit felt so right with her. I would give her time to cut her nigga off, but she had a time limit. If she didn't do it by the time I wanted her to, I was going to handle him myself.

16

MICAH

Before I could go back home, I stopped to get Leikyn some food. I planned to have her locked away with me until she had to go back to class. We had some making up to do, well I had making up to do.

I stopped in Cajun Seafood Market and just my fuckin' luck Tasha was in there. I walked right by the table she was sitting at and went to counter. I had to pull my phone out to look at Leikyn's text of what she wanted.

"Let me get uhhh— a pound of lobster tail, New Orleans style, and two snow crab leg dinners."

"$45.53," the cashier said a little too happy to take my money.

"Hungry ass girl," I mumbled and sat down.

"So, you just gon' act like you don't see me?" Tasha brought her ass over and sat across from me.

"Yeah, that was the plan, I would think you got the hint."

"I can't believe you let your little girlfriend put her hands on me, then you didn't even have the decency to check on me," Tasha spat.

"Bi— you breathing, ain't you? Now unless you want part

two of that ass whooping, you need to go head and go back over there." I pointed to the table she just came from.

"Order 82." Tasha got up and grabbed her food. Before she stormed out the door she shot a look that I guess was supposed to scare me.

"Something wrong with that hoe," I mumbled to myself.

"Here you go, sir." The cashier handed me the food all bagged up.

"Whatever. Butter and sauce come with this shit in here, right? 'Cause I ain't coming back if you fucked up, you bringing it to me."

"I'll just give you some extras," she nervously chuckled and started putting a bunch of stuff in a smaller bag. "Have a good day."

I tipped them before I left out. I checked my surroundings as I made my way to my truck. I felt like that crazy bitch Tash was gon' pop up and make me shoot her ass.

"Mic, I hope my food not cold fo' real," Leikyn popped off before I could even lock the door.

"You better be lucky I went and got yo' ass something."

"Nigga, you could've let me finish my date and I would've eaten good."

"Leikyn, keep playin' like I'm a joke and I'm gon' hurt you. I should go split ol' boy shit since you think it's a game." I turned to leave back out the door and she sprinted her ass off the couch.

"Miiiicccc, stop playing," Lei whined and pulled on my arm. I looked over her and she was out of that tight shit she had on before, and in one of my shirts.

"You better be sharing some of that lobster," I told her as we walked to the dining table.

We ate, and this was the only time it was quiet in the house. If I didn't have my dick buried in her or was stuffing her face with food, she was wildin' on me. When we started this shit, I was cool with that crazy shit, but it's time to chill. Especially with this new position we are getting put in, I couldn't have my lady out here loose.

∞

Some shit was going on with Leikyn and she was trying to hide it from. Last night she was on the phone with Sameerah and had to step out the room to finish talking. When we start doing that?

Then she rushed out today, talking about she had to go study with Sameerah and she'll see me later. If we didn't have this meeting today, I would've followed her ass around. I'll be damned if I'm out here being faithful only for her to be playin' me out in the end.

"A'ight, listen up niggas, I know we told you about the trip to Colombia me and Mic got to make, but plans have changed. I'll need a few of y'all to go with us because we expect some static out there." Levi sat at one end of the table and I was on the other.

"We all need to go and show mothafuckas how we get down," one of our soldiers hyped up, probably trying to look good since Les was in attendance.

"You stupid nigga then who gon' watch the money we got here?" I asked, watching his ball up in confusion. "Right, you ain't think that far ahead, that's exactly the type of nigga I want far away from me," I spat.

"Like I was saying. We got a couple of guys to travel with us but you going by boat to make sure our weapons get where they need to go. If you happen to fuck this up, then you signing your own death certificate."

"Any questions?" We looked around the room and was met with head nods.

"If we expect war overseas, you know to be cautious on

the home front. If anything look suspicious, you better dead it, I'm not taking no L's."

"We got an open route from Tampa to Cartagena, so it'll be smooth sailing," Les spoke from the corner.

That concluded the meeting and niggas left to go pack a bag and wrap up whatever they needed before leaving. That trip was going to take at least five days, so they were leaving asap to have everything set up and ready when we arrived.

"Man, I got hit up the mall, a nigga needs something clean for this trip," I said, rubbing my hands together.

"Hell yeah, we can slide together; I need to do the same."

"Bet." I nodded to the niggas that was left behind and made my way out to my truck. Levi hopped in with me and I peeled off to Lenox Square. I whipped my truck in a spot and hopped out.

"Damn them bitches nice other there," Levi pointed, nodding to the Tesla dealership we passed.

"Hell yeah but a nigga like me can't be caught out here charging my whip and shit. That's a jack boy's dream," I laughed.

"True, can't have her out here like that."

"Nigga who? Sameerah?"

"You already know." Levi got this goofy ass grin on his face when I mentioned Sameerah's name.

"Let me find out my son in love," I joked.

"I ain't say all that, but I fuck with shorty," Levi tried to downplay the shit.

"Bro, you over here mentally picking out eighty thousand dollars cars, you more than fuck with her. I commend you for settling down."

"Damn, if I wanted to get a prep talk on love, I would've invited Pops."

"Fuck you."

We were getting our grown man shit on during this trip,

so we grabbed a few pieces from Armani Exchange and Brooks Brothers. I need some new ice for my wrist, so I made a detour to my jeweler. I grabbed a matching set for Leikyn that cost more than the Cartier watch I got for myself.

"Where I'm taking you?" I asked Levi once we were back in traffic.

"To my ride so I can go snatch my girl from my blocking ass sister."

"Sayless." I wasn't about to debate the shit because I wanted my girl to myself. I sent her a text while I was at a red light.

Me: Wrap up that lil' study session and meet daddy at home.
Wife: It better be some food waiting for me or I'm staying home.
Me: Have yo' fat ass at home in an hour.
Wife: Home, huh?
Me: Hell yeah, you need to stop playing and move all the way in.
Beep! Beep!

"Fuck you!" I yelled out the window at the mothafuckas honking at me.

Levi was so deep in his phone, he ain't notice we damn near sat through a green light either. I already knew he was texting lil' sis, so I wasn't even about to cap with him. He can play that 'we chillin" card all he wants but homie nose was wide open.

I dropped Levi off and went to check on the money before heading to the crib. I been calling and texting Leikyn's lil' ass and she was screening my calls. When I didn't see her car parked in the driveway, I kept going to her house. I got too used to sleeping next to her at night for her to pull this.

I whipped in behind Leikyn's car and jogged to the door. I used my key to let myself in and found her laid across the couch with a bowl of popcorn. When she noticed me standing there, she didn't even blink my way.

"Yo, why you here?" I asked, still standing in the doorway of the living room.

"Because I live here," she said with a roll of her eyes.

"Come on, Ma; I got too much shit on my plate to be doing this right now. Tell me what I did so we can get over it."

"That's your fuckin' problem, Micah! You think I'm going to just keep dealing with shit from bitches over you? I don't mind smacking hoes every day but it damn sure won't be over yo' dog ass." Leikyn flung her entire bowl of popcorn at me and I ducked before I got hit in the damn head.

"What the fuck is wrong with yo' crazy ass, you on yo' period?"

"You! I'm tired of this!" Leikyn broke down in tears and I was stuck. I was used to seeing all kind of emotions from this crazy ass girl, but to see how hard she was crying had me thinking I really did something.

"Ssshh, baby, don't cry. I'm sorry. Whatever I did, I'm sorry." I eased next to Leikyn and rubbed her back. I ain't gone lie; I was scared to sit down next to her. This girl was really crazy and would've stabbed me when I was close enough.

After a few minutes, Leikyn calmed down and put some space between us. "Look, I'm trying to be a better person and that don't include dealing with yo' hoes. Mic, you know me and I'm not about to be in no competition with her," Leikyn sniffled.

"I'm sitting here telling you I don't know what you talkin' 'bout, and I'm serious. I ain't been fucking with nobody, but you and I thought I showed you that."

"So, this Tasha bitch is just delusional and like getting her ass beat? Because if you tell me that, then I can go put her out her misery right now." Leikyn threw the cover off her body and jumped up.

"Calm down. you not about to be out here on no wild shit, I'll handle it. Now put your shit on so we can go home, please." Leikyn stared at me with her arms folded across her chest before storming off to her room.

Sighing, I pushed my dreads on my face and laid my head back. This bitch Tasha wasn't this much of a headache when I was actually fucking her.

"I'm ready, and I hope you plan on feeding me."

"You know daddy gon' take care of you. Why you think that ass spreading like that?" I smacked her hard on the ass and followed her outside. I planned on feeding and fucking her all night, that she didn't have to worry about.

17

SAMEERAH

My hands quivered as I fixed a peanut butter and jelly sandwich. It was finals day, and all I could think about was whether Lei and I would pass or not.

We were so close to the finish line, I could taste it. Everything depended on today. Whether we would receive our degrees and step foot into a new life. The way we had studied, I was confident we could.

My phone buzzed on the counter, showing I had two messages. One was from Lei, informing me she was on her way. God knew I was so thankful for my best friend. It had been rough not having my own transportation, but thanks to her and Levi, I got where I needed to be. They alternated taking me to work and anywhere else I needed to be when I wasn't with Levi, which was always. I couldn't help it. I loved being around him.

The second message was from Levi, wishing me well on my finals. I smiled as I read the text over and over. He truly cared about my future. I texted him back and laid my phone back down to finish making my sandwich.

As I took my first bite, I heard the front door shut and rolled my eyes. Taizere dragged his feet across the floor and into the kitchen where I was leaned against the counter. Things between us had been different, especially after I had sex with Levi.

I wouldn't allow Taizere to touch me. I only wanted to feel Levi stroking my insides. Every time I thought about it, I knew it was wrong, but I couldn't help myself. I was addicted to Levi. I just didn't have the heart to break things off with Taizere. I didn't want to leave him stranded after he'd been leaning on me for so long. I wouldn't want him doing it to me.

I studied his appearance, and he looked rough. Lack of sleep had him looking a few years older than what he was. Bags rested underneath his eyes as he looked me up and down. I didn't know what he was thinking, but I was sure it wasn't good, and I didn't have time for it. I needed to be in a good, mental head space for finals. He ruined it the second he opened his mouth.

"Oh, you're home," Taizere started, chuckling lightly. "What nigga been keepin' you, Meerah? I bet it is Lei's bitch ass brother, huh? The nigga who dropped you off that day, right? Y'all looked really friendly together."

His question caught me off guard. I almost choked on the ball of bread in my mouth. His menacing glare scared me.

I couldn't see how he realized I was gone so much when he was gone more than me. I could spend an entire day with Levi, and still make it home before Taizere. He would take money from my wallet to catch an Uber to the studio every day, if that was where he was going. He was just walking in the house from after being gone for over fifteen hours, but wanted to hound me about being gone all the time? I was over it.

"You've got to be kiddin' me, Zere? I should be the one questionin' you on what hoe been keepin' you!" I yelled, finding my voice. Being around Levi's rude ass had me speaking my mind more. Shock was written all over Taizere face as he mugged me.

"You know I'm always in the studio workin'! I been workin' my ass off day and night to make bread for us. You see what fuckin' time it is? I been in the studio since yesterday tryin' to get shit right."

"Where's your album, Zere? Where's the money? I haven't seen either, and I'm becoming fed up. I've been holdin' the house down since day one. You say you're working, but don't have anything to show for it. I don't understand. How could you be in the studio day and night with no result? This has been going on for years. I'm at school and work all day, and I sure as hell have something to show for it."

"Excuse me? I don't think I heard you correctly."

"You heard me. I don't have time for this today. I have finals today, and I don't need your mess interfering with my thought process. I can't keep doin' this, Zere. Either step up and be a man, or I'm gone. Your choice."

My heart and mind were already made up. I was done with him, but I felt I owed it to him to give him a chance to get his shit together. Whatever decision he made would affect us.

Taizere stormed over to me, wrapping his large hand around my neck. Stunned in fear, I glared at him with wide eyes as he pressed me against the counter. I'd never seen him look so deranged, and I honestly feared for my life.

"Who do you think you're talkin' to? That nigga got you feelin' yourself?" he accused through gritted teeth, squeezing harder. I gasped for air, shaking my head no. "You know how I am, Meerah. I don't appreciate the way you been actin' lately. You let that nigga get my pussy? Huh?"

"Zere... I... I can't..."

"You unfaithful lil' bitch. After everything we've been

through, you go out and open yo' legs for another nigga? I ain't stupid, Meerah. I smell that muthafucka on you when you come in. I guess Leikyn's hoe ass startin' to rub off on you, huh?"

I couldn't speak. The words were caught in my throat right along with all the air I had. Taizere had a far off look in his eyes as his grip became tighter and tighter. My body became weak. My eyes rolled into the back of my head. Taizere was still talking, but I couldn't hear anything he said. I thought I would pass out until he let me go and I dropped to the floor. Gasping for air, I thought it was over, but I was wrong. Next thing I felt was a burning sensation in my scalp as he pulled my hair, making me look up at him.

"Please, Zere," I begged. "I'm sorry."

"Oh, so you admit you fucked that nigga?"

"I... I didn-"

My sentence was cut short with his closed fist connecting to my mouth. I instantly felt my lips split open and blood trickle down my chin. I couldn't believe he had hit me. He took his abuse to a new level, and I refused to keep myself in the relationship. I tried giving him a chance, but he ruined it. Taizere went to strike me again, and I bawled up in fear. I waited for his blow, but instead, I heard him cry out.

"Aaaghhh!"

"Stupid muthafucka! Hit me, bitch!" Lei yelled.

I looked up to see she had hit him over the head with the vase full of flowers I had on my table. Taizere laid out on the floor, holding the back of his bleeding head. Quickly, I shot up and ran to Lei. Before I made it to her, she pulled her taser out and shoved it right up his balls. His body shook terribly as she sent all the electric bolts through his body.

"That's enough, Lei! Think about the baby," I expressed, touching her shoulder. I knew how she got down, and she would keep going in on Taizere.

"Nah, fuck this nigga, Meerah! Look at what the fuck he did to your face! I swear Levi gon' put his mark ass in the dirt!"

"Come on. Let's go. I don't want to be here anymore."

Tears welled up in my eyes as I felt my lips throb and swell. I wanted to blame myself for him hitting me, but I knew better. I was wrong for cheating on him. Still, it didn't mean he could put his hands on me.

Lei let up, kicking him in the balls. I sent a few kicks to his stomach, letting out some of the rage brewing inside me. When I was satisfied, I gathered my things and we left.

"Look at yo' fuckin' lip, Sameerah! Why the fuck did he hit you?"

Sighing, I pulled her mirror down and observed my lips. It was busted bad, and I felt I would need stitches. For now, I would need an ice pack to place on it until we were finished with finals. I didn't care how bad of a morning I had; I was determined to pass. It was the only thing that mattered to me.

I rambled the events of my morning to Lei, pausing for her dramatic comments. She was heated, and so was I. I begged her to let me tell Levi. She would slip and tell him about Taizere's other abusive ways, and I wasn't ready to talk about them yet. She stopped by the store and got me an ice pack. It stung and soothed my lip.

"You know you're not goin' back there, right? Hell nah. You're stayin' with me from now on. I don't trust that his bitch ass won't try anything again," she huffed, parking in front of the school.

"I didn't plan on going back. I can't, Lei. He might kill me next time. He almost choked me to death before he hit me," I revealed, and she screamed. "Calm down, Lei. The baby."

"Girl, I'm liable to say fuck this baby to get Taizere's ass. I can't believe he did that to you. It's cool, though. Wait until you tell Levi."

"Come on. I don't want to think about this right now. We need to think about passing these finals."

Nodding, she agreed, but I could tell she was pissed. I truly wanted her to calm down for the baby. She couldn't get so worked up over things like she used to. My bestie had another life to think about.

We said a quick prayer before getting out and going to our classes. Finals last well over four hours, and I was so thankful when they were over. Our professors promised to have grades posted by the weekend, so I would be a wreck all week wondering if we passed or not. Lei and I met up in the middle and walked to her car together. A familiar car was parked next to hers and I knew exactly who it was. Before I could do anything, Lei took off running.

"Brother! Look what the fuck that nigga did to Meerah's lip!" she yelled to Levi, who stepped out the car looking good enough to eat. He had a fresh haircut, and I loved the way his beard was lined up. I couldn't bask in how good he looked because of Lei's big ass mouth.

Levi marched over to me and pulled me into him. Gripping my chin, he studied my face. He ran his finger over my lip, gritting his teeth in anger.

"That fuck nigga did this to you?"

"Annnddd, he choked her out! I tasered that muthafucka until he was foamin' at the mouth," Lei added, getting hype again.

"Where he at now?" Levi asked me.

"I... I don't know."

"Let's go find him," he demanded, pecking my lips and grabbing my hand. "Lei take yo' rowdy ass home and stay there."

"Give me some money, so I can get some food, then."

"Here, man."

"Thank you," she snatched the money from him. "Take care of my best friend, Levi. I won't hesitate to taser yo' ass, too."

"Man get on. I got my baby."

Lei hugged me and made me promise I would text her every hour. I knew she worried, but not as much when I was with Levi. I whispered in her ear for her to keep calm for my godchild. I swear I loved her crazy ass.

I hopped in the car with Levi and he pulled off. He swerved in and out of traffic, driving like a bat out of hell. His knuckles were white from holding the steering wheel so tightly. His jaw was clenched, and his eyes were low. I didn't know what to say, so I reached over and took one of his hands in mine. Some of the tension left his body, but not much. He kissed the back of my hand and peered at me.

"How long he been doin' that shit, Sameerah?"

"Doin' what?"

"Don't play stupid, man. How long that nigga been puttin' his hands on you? And, don't lie to me."

"Honestly, this was the first time he's actually hit me. Usually, it's small, hurtful things to leave bruises. Today, he went over the edge."

"Explain to me what happened."

For the second time that day, I explained Taizere's actions. Levi listened intently, nodding his head every so often. By the time I was finished, we were pulling up in front of my house. Levi could barely park the car before he hopped out, demanding I stay inside. Out the corner of my eye, I saw Micah's car park beside us and I knew shit was about to get ugly. Micah hit me with a head nod and followed Levi inside my house.

Impatiently, I waited for them to come back out. When they did, I gasped at the sight before me. Levi held onto a bruised and battered Taizere as Micah held a gun to his head. I thought I would feel bad for Taizere, but I didn't. He deserved whatever they did to him. Levi knocked on the car window, instructing me to get out. Hesitantly, I did, walking around the front of the car.

"Say what the fuck you gotta say," Levi barked to Taizere, who looked to be barely breathing. His lip matched mine with much more damage to his eyes and nose. His breathing was off, and I wondered did he need to get to a hospital.

"I... I'm so... sorry, Meerah," Taizere stammered, spitting out blood.

"Do you accept his apology, lil' sis? If not, I can send him to his maker," Micah pressed, cocking his gun.

"No, no. I accept it. Can we please just leave? I don't want to be here, Levi."

"A'ight. Get back in the car and wait for me."

I did as I was told, but not before stealing one last glance at Taizere. I couldn't believe what we had come to.

I watched as Levi and Micah spoke to Taizere before throwing him to the ground and stomping him out. They dapped each other up, leaving Taizere in the middle of the yard. Levi got back in the car, breathing heavily.

"Take one last look at that nigga, Lil' Black Girl. You won't be seein' him again," he stated, starting his car up.

"I'm scared, Levi," I admitted. "What if he comes back here when I'm alone?"

"You won't be here. You're comin' to live with me. I don't trust that muthafucka, and if it wasn't for you, his brains would be splattered all over yo' yard. Let him keep that house until the landlords kick him out. Is everything in yo' name?"

"Yes."

"A'ight. We'll handle that, too. I got you, Sameerah."

"Can I go inside and get the things I need? I don't have everything with me."

"Only grab important shit. We can get you new clothes and all the other necessities."

Levi followed me inside where I got important papers and things I would need. It was bittersweet knowing I would no longer stay at my house, but I felt it was time for a new start. Too many bad memories lined the wall of that house. I walked right past Taizere, who was passed out. The neighbors would called someone when they saw him.

When we made it to Levi's, he doctored my lip. I was drained, and it was a little past noon. We showered, ate, and sexed until I fell asleep in his arms.

At that moment, everything felt so right. He was where I needed to be.

∞

Levi was gone, but he'd left me the keys to one of his cars, so I wouldn't be stuck in the house. I was up early and fully dressed. I didn't have work, and school was over, so I decided to go see my mother. I was finally giving in. I prayed I wasn't making the wrong decision. It seemed to be all I did lately.

Once I was ready to go, I hopped in Levi's Audi and headed to *Atlanta Breakfast Club*. My lip throbbed, and I hated to be seen with a fat lip, but I couldn't ignore my mother any longer. My palms were sweaty as different scenarios of how our meet would go went through my head. I wanted everything to go smoothly. I wanted my mother to be clean and healthy. I was tired of seeing her at her worst. If she pulled her normal stunt, then I would cut her off for good; something I didn't want to happen.

To calm my nerves, I called Lei.

"Meerah, it better be an emergency for you to be callin' at the crack of dawn," she groaned.

"It is," I giggled. "You'll never believe what I'm about to do."

"If it has anything to do with my brother, don't tell me. I don't need to know details about how freaky y'all are."

"We're not you and Micah, but no. I'm headed to see my mother."

"Are you sure that's a good idea? You know how it always ends."

"I know, and if it ends the same as always, I'm cutting ties with her too. I don't need toxic people in my life, especially not on this new journey I'm taking."

"I hear you, boo. Be strong, Meerah. I know how you can be weak for her. I understand because she's your mother, but I hate seein' you hurt in the process. Don't even talk to her if she doesn't look clean, okay?"

"Okay," I agreed as I parked into a space. "Well, I'm here. I'll call and let you know what happens."

"How about I call you? I need to sleep in longer."

Laughing, we said our goodbyes and hung up. I sat in the car for three minutes, giving myself a pep talk. I tried to mentally prepare myself for what would happen.

Taking a deep breath, I got out and locked up Levi's car. I went inside and spotted my mother in a booth in the corner. My heart swelled at how good she looked, and I mean really good. I'd never seen her look so healthy. Her face was full and clean. Her stomach had a slight pudge, and her clothes were clean. She looked around the room and our eyes met. Her cheeks rose as she gave me a warm smile. I glided over to her, embracing her tightly.

"It's so good to see you, Mee Mee. I didn't think you would ever give me a chance," she expressed, sniffing.

"I was scared, Mama. You need to understand why I was hesitant. It's because of you," I stated honestly. I pulled away from her, wiped my face, and took my seat across from her.

She looked ashamed, and that was exactly how she needed to feel.

"I don't know what to say, but I'm sorry."

"You can say a lot more than that. You owe me so much more than that."

Lowering her head, she nodded and chewed her bottom lip. She looked amongst the crowded restaurant before reverting her attention to me. Her lower lip trembled as she shook her head.

"I let it beat me, Sameerah. I wasn't strong enough to fight it. The times I did try, it was because of you. I would think about you and how much of your life I missed out on because I was high. It made me feel disgusted with myself, but every time... every time I went back. The withdrawals pained my body. The thoughts of myself made me want to stay high, so I wouldn't think of how fucked up I was," she cried, pausing to get herself together. "Honestly, I don't have an excuse, except for I was weak, and I did what I wanted to do. I should have made you a priority. I was so selfish, Mee Mee. I was so, so selfish. You needed me. I know you did."

"Of course, I did. You're my mother. There were a lot of things I had to learn on my own. I had to take care of you, Mama. I had to grow up way before my time to save my own life. To save your life too. It wasn't fair to me. It's not fair to me. You've missed out on the best years of my life. Hell, all the years of my life. Years you can't get back. In two weeks, if I passed my finals, I will be walking across the stage for a second time. I made it this far without you. Why change when I have it all figured out?" I scoffed, shaking my head. I didn't think I would be upset. I thought I would be happy to see her and to hear her confess her reasonings. It didn't do anything but piss me off.

"I realized I couldn't live my life without you any longer. I realized so much, baby. I need you."

"I need some time to think things over, Mama. I love you and I'm happy to see you healthy and clean. It looks good on you."

Reaching over, I touched her hand and smiled. I didn't have anything left to say. I got up and left, leaving her there to marinate in my words. Deep down, I worried my actions would cause her to relapse. I prayed they didn't, but if so, she wasn't truly clean to begin with.

18

LEIKYN

I was fuming when I left the school. That nigga Taizere better be lucky I didn't have my gun because I would've proudly shot his ass then took my tests like nothing happened. I was so happy when I saw Levi sitting outside because I knew Sameerah would've tried to hide it for as long as she could.

Shaking those negative thoughts off, I made my way to Zaxby's to get some food. I know I needed to slow down eating all day before I can't fit these bikinis I bought for the trip. But all those thoughts flew out the window when my stomach started growling like I haven't ate in years.

I can't believe I had a whole human growing in my stomach. I don't know who I was more scared of telling between my daddy and Levi. The one thing I never wanted to do was to disappoint my daddy; I was his little princess.

The more I thought about it, the more I started to panic. What the hell am I going to do with a baby right now? I'm barely out of college, and even though money wasn't an issue, I don't know if I was ready for that responsibility. What if I was a terrible mom and I messed my baby up for life? That was the type of thing I worried about. Not to mention the life Micah was living isn't ideal to bring a baby in the equation. Hell, we never even talked about having kids.

My phone rang snapping me from my thoughts and Micah's name popped up.

"Hey baby," I answered with a mouth full of fries.

"Damn yo' fat ass stay eating," Micah laughed, making me drop my fry back down. "What you on?"

"Nothing," I said dryly. Just that fast my mood was ruined. If only he knew I was eating so much because of his weak ass pullout game.

"Look, I'm on my way to handle some shit, but I won't be in late, a'ight? Love you."

"Mmmhhmm, love you too." I hung up just as I pulled up to the house. I parked and made sure I had everything. After throwing my trash away I went to the bedroom, stripping out my clothes the whole way.

I laid across the bed and flipped the tv on, so I can take a nap. I couldn't sleep when it was too quiet, but if I was already sleep you better shut the hell up. Turning on Netflix, I went to the episode of Queen of The South I left off last. I think I was sleep before the episode even started good.

"I'm gon' make sure I bust it open really good for Mic and make the head sloppy," I heard Micah whisper in my ear.

"Get the hell away from me," I mumbled and swatted at him before rolling over. This nigga played entirely too much, and I was still sleepy. The other day I told him how people remember stuff you that you whisper in their ear when they're sleep, and this is the shit he's been doing since.

"I got a surprise for yo' big head ass so get up and meet me downstairs."

Smack!

128

Micah smacked my ass hard and I felt the bed shift. I wanted to cry and throw a tantrum, but I got my ass up anyway. I emptied my bladder before throwing some shorts on and going to find Micah in this big ass house.

"Mic!" I called out when I made it to the main floor and didn't see him.

Making my way to the kitchen, I saw the patio door open. I walked out to see Micah was outside trying to start the fire pit but was failing miserably. There was also a table with candles and champagne sitting next to the chaise I laid on.

"Help me do this shit while you over there laughing." Micah looked at me with his face frowned.

"Well, if you take all that wood out of there it would catch better," I giggled. Micah followed my direction and had the fire going after a minute. "What's all this for?" I asked.

"Showing you how much I love and appreciate you, and to congratulate you for getting that degree." My heart was beating a mile a minute the closer Micah got to me.

"I didn't get the degree yet; I got to get my test results."

"You got that shit, baby, stop flexin', and if you didn't, we gon' find that professor and keep taking the shit over until you pass it." I laughed, but deep down I knew he was dead serious.

Micah poured us both a glass before handing me mine. I took a fake sip before sitting it back down. I wasn't ready to tell him about the possible baby yet and didn't want him questioning why I wasn't drinking. Micah threw his cup back before pouring him another. When he brought the pre-rolled blunt from behind his ear, my antennas went up.

"Okay Mic, for real, what's going on?" My breathing was labored because I just knew I was about to spazz if he said something I didn't want to hear.

"You know I love you, right?" When those words left his

lips, I hopped up from my seat. "What you jumping up for? Chill."

"Micah, I swear if you're about to say you got a bitch pregnant or got a secret wife I'm about to go in yo' shit," I warned with my fist balled. Micah took a step towards me and I moved back.

"Get the fuck over here, Lei," Micah demanded and snatched me by the front of my shirt. "The only crazy mutha-fucka that's going to carry my last name is your ass, and I got this to prove it to you." Micah brought a small velvet box from his pocket and I held my breath.

"This not an engagement ring, so don't get all crazy and shit, but it's a step. Once we let this out to yo' people, then we can work on something bigger and plan the wedding of your dreams." A few tears slipped from my eyes and Micah smoothly wiped it away.

This is it, bitch, tell him about the possibility of you being pregnant! I was screaming at myself when Micah slipped the ring on my hand. I should've told him right then, but my words were lost. Instead, I just said, "I love you too." and jumped in his arms.

I wrapped my legs around his waist, my arms around his neck, and kissed him sloppily. Micah pinned me against the brick wall and I fumbled with his belt to release his monster. "I had a whole night planned," Micah mumbled against my lips.

"Fuck that, I want some dick," I moaned. With Micah's thick veiny member in my hands, I led it to dripping center.

"Fuucck," Micah groaned as he moved in and out of me slowly. I used his shoulders as leverage as I moved up and down matching his thrusts. The harder he pumped, the more I tried to keep up, not even caring about the wall scratching my back up.

Micah snatched me from the wall, holding me by the ass

so I wouldn't fall. He fucked me silly, never missing a beat while I screamed to heaven, thanking God for this dick. When he finally let go inside of me, we both were breathing like we ran a marathon.

"That shit extra wet, we gotta take this inside and finish. Neighbors probably about to send the laws over here how you screaming," Micah joked. He put me back on my feet and I could barely stand up straight.

"Shut up. I'm about to go back to sleep, I don't know about you— ahh!" Micah swooped me up bridal style and rushed in the house, taking the stairs two at a time.

"Yeah, I'm about to put you to sleep," he smirked cockily. And that's exactly what the hell he did.

I woke up the next morning and I could barely move how sore I was. I don't know what got into Micah, but he was bending and folding me into positions I didn't even know was possible.

"Damn!" I said to myself in the mirror when I saw my hair. My weave was balled up on top of my head, and the part from my frontal was on the wrong side. Thankfully me and Meerah had appointments today. I was gon' have to Debo somebody out the chair. Not even bothering to do too much to my head, I put it in a messy bun before turning the shower on. I stared at my ring all smiles before washing up.

I was about to get dressed for the day and Micah was still snoring in the bed. I placed kisses on his face before grabbing my phone. I texted Sameerah since I hadn't heard from her last night.

Me: Climb off my brother's dick and get dressed! We got appointments lol

*Meerah: I wish I was on it *tongue out emoji**

Me: Please spare the details. I'll be there in thirty minutes.

She knew if I said thirty minutes, that really meant an hour. I put my phone down and went to the walk-in closet for something to wear. I settled on some biker shorts and a matching crop top. My stomach growled as I passed the kitchen, but I was going to grab something on my way. Trekking down the stairs, I was froze in place at what I was looking at.

"MICAH!" I yelled and stormed back in the house. "Micah! This bitch got me messed up," I ranted and fumbled with my phone. I don't even know who I was calling.

"What happened?" Micah came running down the stairs with his gun and damn near tripped.

"This bitch keyed my car and I'm gon' kill her! You said you was gon' handle this shit, Mic," I fumed as I paced the floor. Micah took off outside in his boxers and I was right behind him. He was standing between our cars with his hands on top of his head.

"Shit man!" Micah cussed and walked around his truck. My attention was stuck on the damage to my car; I didn't even see that his tires were flat too.

"I got shit to do today so what's shakin'?" I asked with my hand propped on my hip.

"Take my truck that's in the garage and I'll get this fixed."

"I don't want to drive that big ass truck with the three rows. Got me feeling like a soccer mom and shit. I thought you was handlin' this hoe. What happened? Do I need to pay her another visit?"

"A'ight, Lei damn!" Micah stormed past me and I looked at him like he lost his mind.

"Don't be yelling at me, nigga, you the one got bitches messing my stuff up. The fuck. You better be lucky I got shit to do today or I'll go find that weak hoe," I went on as I snatched the keys and got in the truck.

It took me fifteen minutes to get to Levi's house and Sameerah came right out. "Ooohh this something new from

Mic?" Sameerah asked when she got inside. The swelling on her lip went down a lot and I was glad.

"No, this is something to drive because Micah's side hoe decided to mess my baby up. I swear the bitch just can't take a hint." I shook my head as anger radiated through me.

"Just calm down ,Lei, that's some material stuff I'm sure has been replaced already." Leave it to Sameerah to want to be the voice of reason when I was ready to go wreck shit.

"Where we going?" Sameerah finally asked as we were riding in silence for a while.

"To check and see if I'm really about to be somebody's mama before I go to jail." Thoughts of the possible baby in my stomach was the only thing stopping me from tracking this bitch Tasha down right now. I know it was her ass because I didn't have problems with nobody else.

"Ooohh Yaaay! I'm so excited. Did you tell Mic yet?"

"No, I'm not telling anybody nothing until I figure out what I'm going to do," I sighed.

"What you mean by that?" Sameerah looked at me like I had three heads or something.

"I mean, having a baby is a big deal, Meerah, and I'm not one hundred percent sure that this is what I want for my life right now."

"Girl, you talking crazy now," she waved me off and started typing away on her phone.

When I pulled up to the Ob/Gyn, I was nervous. While I signed myself in, Sameerah found us some seats. It seemed like every pregnant person in Atlanta had appointments today, all you saw were big bellies everywhere.

"Leikyn Hart," a nurse called my name and I jumped up quick with Sameerah right behind me. The nurse took my height, weight, and gave me a cup to pee in. Now it was the waiting game for the doctor to come in.

"Knock, knock. Hi Leikyn, I'm Dr. Leary. What can I do

DEEANN & AJ DIX

for you today?" A middle-aged black woman came strutting in
with her folder in her hand.

"I need to know if I'm pregnant or not," I simply said
with a shrug.

"Well, you are definitely pregnant according to the urine
sample you gave. When was your last menstrual cycle?"

I had to sit and think because I really couldn't remember
when it was. "Maybe last month, I don't even remember
honestly. We just got done with finals, and everything has
been overwhelming, so I can't give you a date." I held my
head down in embarrassment. I felt Sameerah's small hand
rubbing my back.

"Let's take a look. Lie back for me." I did what she said
and laid back on the table.

For some reason when she got the ultrasound machine
and put it on my stomach, I turned my head away. Dr. Leary
already confirmed that I was, in fact, pregnant, but I felt
seeing it would make it real.

Sameerah gasped and I quickly turned to look at the
screen. "What happened? Something's wrong with the baby?"
I panicked.

"Nope, everything looks perfectly fine right now. You look
to be about thirteen weeks, give or take a few days."

"Oh my— it's a little alien inside of me." I got emotional
seeing the little spec on the screen and looked to see
Sameerah wiping her eyes too.

"Like I said everything looks good, just make sure you
take the prenatal vitamins I prescribe and come back in four
weeks for a follow-up. Congratulations." Dr. Leary printed
me a picture of the baby before leaving us in the room.

"It's real, bestie," Sameerah spoke, breaking me from my
own thoughts as I stared down at the picture.

"I know, and you better keep your mouth closed to Levi. I
want to enjoy Colombia before I have my second daddy

jumping down my throat." Sameerah agreed and I gathered my stuff to leave.

I stopped at the front desk to get my next appointment before going to the hair salon. I can't believe I'm really about to have a baby.

Shit's about to hit the fan for real.

❧ 19 ❧

LEVI

A nigga was cheesing as I watched my sister and girl graduate college. When they found out they passed all their finals, they cried all night. I left them alone with that shit. I was proud as hell, but I wasn't with the emotional shit.

My parents, Mic, and I all went in on their graduation gifts. I knew exactly what to get Sameerah, but it was hard as hell picking for Lei because her spoiled ass had everything. Ma had the final say over what we got her, and it was something she didn't need, but would be happy as hell with.

Sameerah and Lei ran out the stadium together, holding hands and crying. When they got to us, they hugged one another and bounced up and down. The tight dress Lei wore had me eyeing her. She looked a little pudgy, but it was a round, small pudge. Her gown covered most of it, so no one else noticed. I didn't want to assume shit. Maybe, her ass was just gaining weight.

"I can't believe we did it," Sameerah sang, smiling brightly.

"Me either! It's time to turn uuuppp!" Lei yelled dramatically.

"I'm so proud of you girls," Ma expressed, hugging them both. "I knew you could do it."

"Me too," Pops cosigned.

I let them have their moment with Sameerah. She looked so happy, and that made me smile. My baby accomplished something big. I couldn't wait to reward her for all her hard work.

"Congrats, Lil' Black Girl," I whispered in her ear from behind.

"Thanks," she answered shyly.

"I got something for you."

"What?"

"You feel that?" I chuckled, pressing my hard dick against her ass. She blushed and moved away, turning to face me.

"Really, Levi? Your parents are here," she lowly scolded me.

"You think I give a fuck? I'm grown, bruh."

She just giggled and rolled her eyes. We stood there talking until we got the call their gifts had been delivered to my house. Sameerah and Lei hopped in the car with Mic and me. My parents followed behind us. The girls were so excited they wouldn't shut up. If it was any other time, I wouldn't have allowed it. I wasn't with that yelling and shit all the time, but I tried to understand how they felt.

"Levi, whose cars are those?" Lei shouted, hitting the back of the seat.

Her crazy ass jumped out the second I put my car in park. Sameerah was right behind her, running to the car I had picked out for her. Well, the car she said she would buy when she had the money. It was a cocaine white Lexus IS. That car was bad as fuck, and I knew Sameerah would look good behind the wheel.

She ran her hand over the glossy paint, admiring its beauty. Ma had picked Lei out an Infinity SUV. It matched hers, and I believed that was the only reason she got it.

"Are you guys for real?" Lei screamed, dancing. "Is this mine?"

"Is this mine?" Sameerah breathed in disbelief.

"Nah, it's mine. You can drive it when you want, though," I teased.

"Boy, leave that girl alone. Let her be happy," Ma fussed. "Yes, baby. It's yours. It's a gift from all us."

Sameerah broke into tears while Lei hopped in her ride, bouncing in her seat. I swaggered over to Sameerah and took her in my arms. Her little sensitive ass.

"Thank you," she cried.

"See, this what it's like when you fuck with a real nigga. You deserve to be rewarded for accomplishing your goals."

"Toot toot! Leggo, Meerah! We about to stunt on these hoes, for real," Lei yelled out her window.

"Take yo' ass on, man. You ain't about to have my girl out here actin' like you."

"You hatin', Levi. Meerah ain't worried about you. Niggas about to be checkin' for her after they see her in her new whip."

"Don't get fucked up."

"Watch your mouth, boy. Let that girl breathe and ride in her new car. She'll be back."

"Nah, I'm goin' with her. We can ride the block together."

"You sprung, bruh," Mic clowned me.

"Fu- shut up, Mic. You can ride with Lei non-drivin' ass."

I hopped in with Sameerah and let her drive me all around town. We all ended up stopping to eat and chill. I needed some down time before the trip to Colombia because I knew shit would get hectic the moment we touched down.

∞

The plane ride to Colombia was long as hell, but it gave Mic, and I time to go over the plan again. We decided on bringing ten of our best men along. Pops had shit mapped out for us. He knew how everything worked, so he was the real key to helping us conduct the plan. He had a blueprint of how Mateo's estate looked and profiles on each of Buck's men, including himself. If we moved correctly and precisely, it would be an easy hit.

"What we gon' do with the girls' tomorrow night? You know they gon' want to go to the welcomin' party, but that's a business move. We can't have them around that," Mic stated as we walked a few feet behind them. We were at the resort and the shit was nice. Pops hooked us up. I couldn't wait to see Sameerah's fine ass running around in her swimsuit; even though I preferred her naked.

"Occupy them some other way. I'll find something to hold them over. We don't need them anywhere near that shit."

"I swear these muthafuckas better be on point, or I'm killin' all they asses."

"You know we got them niggas trained well. If one fuck up, that's all their lives. We've drilled the plan in their heads for the last two weeks. Ain't no way they can fuck up."

"Better not."

We took Sameerah and Lei to the suite we would be staying in. Shit was laid out. It had four rooms, three bathrooms, and a view of the beach. Of course, Lei picked the biggest room and I almost kicked her ass out. Sameerah and I needed all the room to fuck around. I planned on being in her guts when I wasn't handling business.

"What you think you doin', Lil' Black Girl?" I questioned her as I saw her choosing a room. I rolled her heavy ass suitcase to the room we'd be staying in together. "I know you didn't think you was about to stay by yo'self. You got shit twisted. You know you stayin' with daddy."

Smiling, she followed me inside the room with the view of the beach. She ran and jumped on the oversized California King bed. The way she was sprawled out made my dick hard. I could easily see up her little ass dress. Her fat pussy lips were trying to eat her boy shorts. Setting our bags to the side, I shut the door and locked it. Mic and I had to head out in a few, but I had the urge to feel Sameerah.

Dropping my shorts and boxers to my ankles, I walked over to her and spread her legs. Her eyes popped open and a smirk tugged at her lips. She knew what it was. Pushing her boy shorts to the side, I eased inside her.

"You were waitin' for this, huh?" I growled. She was wet as fuck.

"Yes," she breathed. "Shit!"

I dug into her walls until Mic's cockblocking ass came banging on the door. Ignoring him, I didn't stop until Sameerah was cumming all on my dick. Seeing her creamy goodness caused me to bust before I wanted to. I cleaned us up and told her I would be back later.

Mic waited for me in the truck waiting outside for us. He looked at me and shook his head. I shrugged. He was hating because he wasn't getting no pussy. The ride to meet Mateo was silent. We didn't want to say much since it was his peoples that scooped us. I studied our surroundings, making note of everything and everyone around us. I noticed some shit my pops talked about. Markers we needed to be aware of. Buck was the enemy in the situation, but I planned on keeping an eye on Mateo too. I didn't trust none of them niggas.

We pulled up to Mateo's estate, and I wanted some shit like it when I got on his status. That muthafucka was living like a true boss. His men led us inside to the meeting room where everyone was in attendance. Mic and I were the last to arrive. I passed everyone and went straight to Mateo who sat at the head of the table. He rose as we got closer, wearing a pleasing smile.

"Gentleman, you are here. It's good to have you," he exclaimed, shaking our hands. "Your father spoke very highly of you. I trust you won't let me down."

"I'm not that type. I'm tryin' to get bread just like you are. I don't play when it comes to what's mine, feel me?" I stated, looking him straight in the eyes.

"We should have no problems, then."

I nodded and let Mic rap with him. Looking around the table, I spotted Buck smirking at me. Muthafucka was funny.

I mugged his ass. I could see he was a sneaky nigga, but I had shit under control. He thought he was about to fuck with us. He was in for a rude awakening.

Mateo introduced us to everyone in attendance. Everyone in the room was a supplier for him in different areas of the states. When he got to Buck, Mic and I walked past him like he wasn't there. I wasn't no fake nigga, so I wasn't about to start acting like one. Mateo chuckled and continued following us around the table.

"Now that almost everyone is acquainted, it's time to talk business," Mateo announced. Two women came around passing out papers and phones. "The paper is your new contract. Once signed, we will discuss shipment dates and orders. The phones are for you to reach me or my right hand, Escobar. That is the only way I am to be contacted. I'll have a one on one with everyone before their flight leaves. Of course, it will be after the welcoming party for Levi and Micah. Everyone is to be in attendance."

It took an hour for the meeting to wrap up. It took his wife barging in and demanding he take her out. Pussy had power because he dismissed us without a second thought. Seemed like some shit I would do for Sameerah.

Mic and I headed out behind everyone. Through the meeting, I was able to get a feel of everyone. No one other than Buck seemed to be off. He grilled Mic and me the entire meeting. I swear it was like we ruined that nigga's life or something with how much hate he gave us. He was one of those old hating ass niggas who hated to see the young ones come up. That jealousy was going to cost him his life.

"You peep how that muthafucka was grilling us?" Mic chuckled, clapping his hands. "He already know what the deal is."

"I'm ready too. He ain't gon' know what hit him."

"Hell nah. I'm gon' chill tonight because I need my head right for this shit."

"I feel you. I'm gon' fuck on Sameerah some more and lay up."

"How you get hooked so fast, bruh? Sis must got some fire ass pussy."

"Aye, watch what the fuck you say, bruh," I warned, mugging his ass. "You better look around for some Colombian pussy."

"I'm good on that. I came to handle business and chill with my peoples."

"Real shit."

We made it back to the resort to find Sameerah and Leikyn at the pool. We went to change and join them. Might as well have fun before catching a few bodies.

20

MICAH

Watching Leikyn in this lil' ass bikini had my dick harder than a mothafucka. She was looking thicker than usual, and I smirked to myself 'cause that was all on me. Sameerah and Levi was all caked up while I had to watch my shorty from a distance like a clown.

"Can we do something besides watch y'all suck each other's face off?" Leikyn rolled her eyes.

"Get out grown folks business, Lei." Levi didn't even bother to look her way as he continued to feel Sameerah up.

"Nah, I'm being a cock blocker right now. If I can't get none, y'all can't either. Let's go find some food." Leikyn stood up and I just watched the water drip off her body. I was just in them guts before we got here, but that wasn't enough to last a week, shit.

"That's all yo' ass think about," Levi mumbled and Sameerah playfully hit his arm. "Aye unless we fuckin', you better keep ya hands to yoself, Lil' Black Girl."

"Y'all niggas tripping. I'm out." I got up from my chair and made my way back to the suite behind Leikyn.

She made it back before me. I went to her room to get me a quickie in, but Leikyn wasn't in her room. "Where this damn girl at?" I wondered as I trekked to my room.

"Took you long enough," Leikyn cooed as she was laid across my bed naked. She had her legs was spread eagle and using two fingers to play with herself.

"You playing a dangerous game." I smirked and locked the room door. I dropped my wet swimming trunks and my dick sprang up like a door stopper.

"Hurry up," Leikyn moaned out. I had to smack her hands down 'cause a nigga was getting jealous.

"Fuck," I groaned in pleasure when I entered my favorite place. It was something different about Leikyn; she was wetter than before and had my mans in a death grip. If I kept looking down in her eyes like I was, this shit was about to be quick.

"Turn yo ass over!"

Smack!

I smacked her ass hard and watched it jiggle. Knowing we had to hurry up, I entered her roughly and start pounding into her spot over and over.

"Yeesss, Mic! Baby, just like that," Leikyn screamed and I had to push her head in the pillow before somebody heard her ass.

"Shut the fuck up, Lei—agh fuck!" She started throwing her ass out and I couldn't hold it any longer. I painted Leikyn's wall with my seed before collapsing on her back.

"Get yo' heavy ass up, nigga; I can't breathe."

"My bad, baby." I moved and placed a kiss on her forehead. Between that long ass flight and Leikyn just draining me, a nigga needed a nap.

"I guess I'll order something for everybody to eat. What you want?"

"It doesn't matter." I had my arms over my eyes, drifting off to sleep.

Leikyn smacked her lips before getting out the bed. "A'ight, don't be looking crazy if you don't like what I get."

"Love you too, bae," I mumbled before sleep welcomed me.

I opened my eyes thinking I took a quick nap and it was the next damn day. I smell some food cooking and could hear Leikyn's loud mouth ass in the kitchen with Sameerah, so I went in there.

"Morning," I spoke, making myself seen.

"About time you got up, nigga, we thought you was dead," Leikyn popped off.

"The food would be ready in a minute. Levi's out on the balcony," Sameerah added with a smile. I thanked her before going to find him.

The smell of some loud smacked me in the face when I slid the door open. "Damn, you out here getting lit without me."

"Bro, yo' ass been sleep since yesterday, I thought you was off the shits." Levi handed me the Dutch and I took a long pull.

"Man, all that hot shit we been on starting to catch up to me. What time we making that move tonight?"

"Shit at like eight. I got Puff and some niggas following Buck to see if he about something. The nigga slick followed us here yesterday but ain't make no moves."

"Them niggas' pussy, I can't wait to peel his shit back," I fumed.

"The food's ready." Sameerah poked her head out the door and said. Levi's face lit up when he saw her, and I just smirked at this in love ass nigga.

"So what y'all got going on tonight?" Levi asked the girls as he bit into his bacon.

"You saying that like y'all about to dip out somewhere." Leikyn cut her eyes at me and I ignored it. This nigga on one.

"We got some business to handle later on, so yeah, we dipping out."

"Now's a fine time to be letting us know. What if we had something planned for us to do? What business you got here?" Leikyn shot off question after question, staring a hole in my head the entire time.

"Exactly," Sameerah added her two cents and folded her arms across her chest.

"Some business that don't involve you tagging along, Lei damn. Learn how to listen."

"First of all, Levi, fuck you because we going. Come on, Meerah, bitch, so we can find something to wear. Is it a color theme? Don't matter I'll wear what I want." Leikyn pushed her plate from in front of her and left the kitchen. Sameerah kissed Levi on the cheek before following behind her.

"Maaaan," I drawled, rubbing a hand down my face. "Yo fuckin' sister crazy as hell, man."

Levi just shrugged and continued to eat. "Just 'cause they get dressed don't mean they'll know where we going."

This nigga was really confident in that shit, but he obviously didn't know his sister like he thought. We tried that sneaking out shit, Levi even fucked Sameerah to sleep thinking his plan was solid. Twenty minutes after we arrived at Mateo's estate, there was commotion outside.

"Let me in this bitch I was invited!" Hearing Leikyn yelling outside all I could do was shake my head and look at Levi before taking off.

"Yo!" Levi yelled over Leikyn's yapping. "Fuck is up? Nigga don't touch them, they with me," he spat at the security, trying to stop Sameerah and Leikyn from coming inside.

"Told you I was invited," Leikyn said then jumped at the

security. We walked back inside, trying not to cause any more commotion. "This don't look like no fuckin' business to me, lying ass nigga."

"Baby, this is business. How you even know where to find this place?" I asked Leikyn.

"I tracked your phone. You embarrassed of me or something, why couldn't I be on your arm tonight, Mic?"

"This is business, but some shit might pop off, and we didn't want y'all in the middle of it," I said as that clown nigga Buck walked in with his people. The nigga looked over at us and I smelled the bullshit in the air. I looked over at Levi, and he peeped it too.

"Aahh, the men of the hour. This is your official welcome to Colombia celebration. Who are these two beauties on your arm?" Mateo approached us with his wife in tow. I didn't know how to introduce Lei, so I was glad when Levi took over.

"This my girl, Sameerah and my baby sis, Leikyn." Mateo kissed the back of both their hands before introducing his wife.

"You two are beautiful, and this one is glowing. Congratulations. How far along are you?"

"Wh—huh?" Leikyn stuttered and looked up at me with wide eyes.

"Fuck she talking about?" Levi asked.

"Um, Leikyn, let's go to the restroom. Which way is it?" Sameerah cut in and grabbed Leikyn away. I was frozen in place watching them walk away.

"I'm sorry. I didn't mean to cause any trouble," Mateo's wife apologized before making herself scarce.

"I guess we have more than one thing to be celebrating tonight." Mateo raised his glass and took a sip. "Let's go to speak in a more private area, gentlemen." Mateo walked off and it felt like there was cement in my shoes as I followed behind him.

Levi was grilling me, but I wasn't thinking about that shit right now. My mind was still trying to wrap around Leikyn being pregnant. Why wouldn't she tell me some shit like that?

The thought of her having a baby by another nigga had me heated, and I was ready to go shake the shit outta her until I got all the answers I needed.

Well," Mateo started, pulling me from my thoughts. "Since we're now in business and I have a lot of respect for your father, I wanted to give you two a heads up. Buck isn't particularly happy with our agreement and he's expressed handling it. Now if you want me to take care of that for you—"

"With all due respect, we got this. Buck is going to get handled, and we'll be back to discuss our expansion in his area before we head back to the states."

"You are not in America, hermano. Don't let your cockiness be the reason something happens to you and those two pretty women you have on your arms."

"You threatening us?" I hopped up from my seat ready to beat the burritos out this nigga.

"Chill, Mic."

"Yeah, *Mic*. There's no threat here; we're all family. I was just offering a solution to your problem."

"We appreciate that, but we got it handled." Levi stood up and straightened his blazer before leaving the office.

I mugged Mateo one last time before following suit. My eyes roamed around the room and I was seeing fire when I saw Buck and Rel, one of his flunkies all in Lei and Sameerah's grill. When that ashy knuckle bitch put his lips on my woman, I lost it.

Wham!

I sent my fist across face and instantly, you can see he was dazed.

"Mic!" Leikyn shrieked and tried to grab my arm. I shook her off and went right back at going in this nigga's shit.

I was beating his ass for touching what's mine and for trying to come at us reckless. It was only so much disrespect I was going to take before I bodied a nigga in here.

"Let's go, nigga!" Levi barked as he pulled me off a badly beaten Rel. I looked around for Buck and that nigga was nowhere to be found.

I grabbed Leikyn and we rushed out to our waiting truck. We all got in the back and the tension was thick as fuck. I was breathing like a bull how mad I was. Leikyn was sitting next to me staring out the window like nothing just happened. Levi was mugging me like he wanted some problems and Sameerah was sitting scared next to him.

"So, you pregnant and wasn't gon' say shit?" I finally asked Leikyn.

Her eyes went to Levi before turning to me. "I was going to tell you, but I didn't know how yet."

"Fuck that shit. Nigga, you been fuckin' my baby sis and ain't even have the decency to tell me? What type of snake ass shit is you on?"

"Levi don't even play me like I'm a gump ass nigga. We all grown as fuck in this bitch. I ain't gotta tell you who sucking my dick."

"Nigga—" Levi rushed me while we were in the back of this little ass truck and snuck me.

"No!" Leikyn screamed as we exchanged blows. Sameerah had to pull Leikyn away because she was trying to get in the middle of us. "Stop it!"

Boom!

Ratatatatat!

Somebody rammed the back of us and gunfire erupted,

halting whatever bullshit was going on in this truck. I rushed to Leikyn and laid on top of her, while Levi grabbed Sameerah. The truck started to swerve before hitting a pole.

"You good? Everybody good?" Me and Levi spoke simultaneously and reached for our heat.

"Stay here," Levi instructed the girls and we hopped out guns ready. The black suburban was smoking and riddled with bullets along with a van that wasn't too far down the road. Another truck pulled up, and we were about to light 'em up until Puff hopped out.

"Y'all good? I tried calling you niggas when we saw them tailing you," he explained before we could ask questions.

"Yeah, we good, make sure this get cleaned up. Throw me yo' keys." Puff tossed Levi his keys and we got the girls out the truck.

The ride back to the suite was quiet as hell and I was glad 'cause if Levi even looked at me wrong, we about to be throwing them bitches again. My damn eye was hurting; I knew that shit was gon' be black tomorrow. He might have to run me that fade again.

Levi pulled up to the suite, and we all piled out, not saying a word. I walked back to my room and heard Levi and Sameerah's room door slam.

"Mic," Leikyn whispered from the other side of my room door. I wasn't going to open it until she started banging on the door.

"What, man?"

"You mad at me?" Leikyn pouted.

"Hell yeah, fuck you thought? Is that my baby?" I asked before getting chopped in the throat.

"Nigga don't play with me asking dumb shit. Who the fuck else baby is it going to be? *You* the one with the friendly dick, mothafucka!"

"Look, we can talk about this in the morning. My damn head pounding and I'm tired. Lay yo' ass down."

I got back comfortable in the bed while did the same. She laid on my chest and I wrapped an arm around her. I love Leikyn ass to death; she is going to be my wife. Hell naw, I wasn't mad about the baby; a nigga just doesn't like surprises. We knew what we were doing when we did it. Les might spazz, but I'll take that.

❦ 21 ❦

LEIKYN

The next morning I woke up sore like I was in the ring with Mayweather. All the events from last night start rushing back to me and I got a little sad. So much was going on and we could've died. Knowing that's the reason Levi and Mic didn't want us tagging along made me feel like shit.

Micah was snoring lightly, so I placed a few pecks on his lips before going to the bathroom. After I emptied my bladder and handled my breath, I went to see if anybody else was woke because I was starving. Sameerah and Levi's room door was closed, so I texted her phone instead of knocking on the door.

Me: Bestie, you up? Come to the kitchen with me.

I saw she read the message and minutes later, she was coming out the room wiping her eyes.

"Morning, babe. How you feeling?" she asked me and took a seat on the stool.

"Like shit. How mad is Levi right now?" Before she could answer, Levi came storming around the corner and didn't even look my way. "Good morning, brother," I said sweetly.

Silence.

"Do y'all want to go sit down and have breakfast? I saw a place not far from here?" Sameerah tried talking to him.

"Nah, I'm good."

"Levi, really? You're just being too damn petty now; I'm telling daddy," I whined and folded my arms around my chest.

"Good, make sure you tell him you being a hoe out here."

I leaned back slightly in my seat because he had me fucked up. "You got me fucked up, I ain't out here being shit but Leikyn Symone." I hopped up and got in his face. Me and Levi fought when we were little and I was ready to relive that shit.

"Come on, Lei, let's not do this, this morning," Meerah urged, standing between the both of us. I left Levi's stupid ass in the kitchen and damn near kicked Micah's room door open. He jumped up from the noise and grabbed his gun that was on the nightstand.

"Damn strong ass girl," he groaned and laid back.

"Micah, get up! Levi is being a real asshole and I'm ready to go in his shit." I paced the floor in front of him.

"That nigga grown as fuck, leave him alone and let him get through that shit. Me and you still need to discuss why you was hiding the shit from me."

"Same reason why you was hiding hoes; because I can! You act like I had the baby and hid it from you, shit I just found out last week."

"That ain't no excuse, Ma. The second you found out you was carrying my seed, I should've been the first person you called. I bet Sameerah knew, didn't she?"

"Yeah, that's my best friend. What's your point?"

"I'm yo' nigga!" Micah's voice raised, making me jump back from him. "I ain't feeling this shit right now; I need some space."

"Have all the fuckin' space you need." I threw my hands

up and went to my own room to get dressed. Since everybody want to act like they retarded this morning, I'll go enjoy breakfast by myself.

"Where you going, Best?"

"To get some food," I mumbled to Sameerah and left the suite. The way I was feeling, I was ready to go my ass home now.

∞

WHAT WAS SUPPOSED TO BE A RELAXING VACATION WITH MY best friend, bro, and bae, turned out to be a shit show. The first day was cool, but it went downhill from there. I should've smacked that lil' Colombian bitch for outing my business like that.

Levi hadn't said nothing to me or Micah the last couple days. Me and Sameerah tried to go and do group shit, but Levi shut it down every time. He took his pettiness to another level when he got another room for him and Meerah. While Mic didn't care, my feelings were hurt. Levi is my big brother and my best friend so for him to be so cold towards me, was painful. The whole plane ride back home was quiet and once we landed, we went our separate ways.

"Bestie call me when you make it in." Sameerah hugged me as Levi walked past like I was invisible. "I'll try to talk to him."

"Fuck him if he wants to be mad then let him I don't care," I lied.

"You're family, he'll get over it; he's just mad and feel betrayed."

Honk! Honk!

Levi rude ass honked the horn for Sameerah.

"Just go before I have to put hands on him." I looked over at Levi and rolled my eyes upward. Mic pulled up moments later and I hopped in his truck. He was still acting like he had a funky ass attitude too and barely said more than a few words to me.

We rode thirty minutes in silence until we pulled up to my house.

"Really nigga, this what we doing?" I looked at him with a scowl.

"Lei just go in the house and I'll hit you when I'm done handling business."

"Fuck you, Micah! You want to sit over here and act like a lil' pussy, don't worry about coming back," I snapped and got out, slamming the passenger door.

"Aye, you forgetting yo' shit," Micah called out from his window he had down.

"Fuck that shit too! I'll have my new nigga buy me and my baby whatever we need." I heard his car door open then close and I picked up my pace to my door. I talked all that cash money shit, but I wasn't trying to be out here fighting with this nigga.

I didn't have to turn around to know Micah was on my ass. I couldn't even get my key in the door before he had a grip on the back of my neck, pushing me to the door. "Keep fuckin' playing them little ass kid games and see I won't run yo' head straight through this house."

"*I'm* playing little kid games?" I asked poking my chest. "You the one that's been ignoring me and shit. You mad because I'm pregnant, nigga? 'Cause I don't need you!"

"No, I'm mad yo' sneaky ass was keeping it from me. You been wildin' out drinking and shit while you carrying my seed? Fuck wrong witchu?"

"I just found out stupid—you know what... I'm not about

to keep doing this back and forth shit with you. Move." I shrugged him off me, so I could unlock my door.

"I'll be back." Micah placed a kiss on my forehead before I could slam the door in his face. This nigga had me fucked up thinking he could handle me any kinda way.

I stormed through my house and flopped on the couch. Here I am bored with no one to talk to because my best friend probably fuckin' my brother right now, and my baby daddy a asshole. Instead of wallowing in pity, I turned on my tv to catch up on the shows I missed while on that fake ass vacation. I ended up dozing off and woke up to my phone ringing back to back. The sun had long gone down but none of those missed calls or texts came from Micah.

I scrolled through Instagram trying to find entertainment in somebody else's drama besides my own. Something caught my attention as I scrolled, and I had to do a double take. This little thirsty broad Tasha posted a picture with Micah in the background. I clicked on her page and there were some live videos with them two. It didn't look like he knew he was being recorded, but that's beside the point. Why the fuck was he out with this hoe instead of being here with me like he was supposed to?

My blood boiled as I watched the video over and over again. Quickly exiting out the app I called Sameerah, and her phone rung a few times before going to voicemail. I called three more times and got the same results.

"Fuck it," I said aloud and went to change into some sweats. You know it's real if I came up out my wig, and that's exactly what I did before wrapping a scarf around my plaits.

I called Micah a few times, and I could tell he was ignoring me because it rang once before he sent it to voice-mail, further pissing me off. I know I said before I was done with Micah dirty ass, but after I whooped him and Tasha's ass one last time, I was wiping my hands with him for real.

Just like in Colombia, I used Find My iPhone to track Micah down. I pulled up to a block in Decatur, and it looked like it was a block party or some shit going on. When I spotted Micah's truck, I whipped and parked any kinda way.

"You want to try to play me, mothafucka?" I fumed as I marched to Micah with my taser in one hand and bat in another. This bitch Tasha was smirking on the side of him like something was funny. I was about to see if she's still smiling after I hit her ass with these 60 million volts and stop her damn heart.

"Lei, fuck is you doing out here?" Micah tried to meet me before I made it to his side hoe, but me swinging my steel Louisville slugger halted his steps. "You wildin'!" Micah yelled and ducked from my swing.

"You and this hoe want to keep fuckin' with me, right?" I yelled and brought my bat down to Micah's windshield. It didn't crack at first, but after a few tries, I finally shattered half of it. I know I probably looked crazy screaming and fucking his ride up, but I ain't care.

When I was about to go apeshit on his back window, Micah rushed me, grabbing me in a bear hug. "Baby, stop! Calm down and think about the baby."

"Get your hands off me," I said calmly. Everything in me was telling me to spit in his face, but I was slick scared.

"I'm gon' let you go, but you need to drop the bat and go. I promise I'll follow behind you, let's go home." Against my better judgment, I let him take the bat from me.

"I'm done," I spat when he let me go. I hopped in my truck and sped off.

My phone started ringing, and Micah's name popped up, I ignored him like he been ignoring me. He called me a few more times before I finally turned it off. I made it home and sat in the car for a while, doing some deep breathing. I saw some headlights pull in behind me, thinking it was Micah.

When I saw three bitches hop out, I just laughed, mad Micah had my bat.

"You got a death wish, bitch," I laughed at this clown and her friends, the same friends that got their asses beat with her before.

"Talk that shit you was spitting now, Micah ain't here!" Tasha yelled as she tried to rush me. I punched that bitch right between her eyes before her friends jumped in. I was fighting like my life depended on it, because in reality, it did, me and my baby's.

I was holding my own until one of them grabbed my hair, bringing me to the ground. I brought Tasha down with me as her friends had me by my hair and kicked me repeatedly. When I felt the first kick in my side, I stopped fighting and balled up in the fetal position. The attack went on for what felt like hours before I heard tires screeching.

"Lei!"

Pow!

Pow!

I recognized Micah's voice as they scattered like roaches. I was in so much pain as I laid on the ground.

"Fuck! Baby, I'm so sorry. Come on and get up." Micah tried to stand me up, but a sharp pain shot through my back, bringing me to my knees. I felt the wetness between my legs and saw the blood stain on my pants.

"Mic, the baby!"

22

SAMEERAH

The ride to Levi's house was silent. He was fuming and had hardly said a word to me since he found out about Lei and Micah.

I couldn't believe how it came out. I'd never seen Lei stunned like that. The expression on Micah's face was pure anger and confusion. Levi's was the same. I felt bad for my bestie, but I had told her the consequences to her actions would catch up to her one day.

"How long they been fuckin' around?" he growled, breaking the silence.

"It's not my place to tell you, Levi. I'm sorry, but they need to be the ones to tell you."

"Fuck that. I ain't got shit for neither one of them. My brother got my sister pregnant, bruh. He been fuckin' my little sister. That shit doesn't sit well with me. If it wasn't for the love I had for them, I swear Mic would be dead. Real shit."

I leaned back and didn't reply. I didn't know what to say. I wanted to comfort him but wasn't sure how he would react.

I'd never seen him so upset. Levi looked so pitiful, in a sexy way. His bottom lip poked out when he wasn't licking or chewing on it.

He wore a deep mug with a hint of sadness and disappointment behind it. I couldn't imagine the pain and betrayal he felt. Mic should have been a man and told him what was happening all along while Levi needed to be man enough to accept it.

We pulled up to his house, and I hopped out. I went to the trunk to get my bags, but Levi quickly dismissed me into the house. I took the keys from him and ran inside. His house felt like home to me. I'd only stayed with him a little while before we went to Colombia, but it felt longer. He had let me add my own little personal touches to his décor and gave me a dresser in his room along with closet space.

Not waiting for him to come inside, I went straight to the bedroom to bathe. I wanted to soak for a long time in very hot water. I needed all the tension relieved from my body, especially after the long flight and dramatic ending of the trip. Turning the water on and pouring some bubbles in, I let it fill the tub as I stripped from my clothes and put my hair in a bun.

"You got in without me? I see how it is," Levi scoffed from the door.

Before I could respond, he ripped off his clothes and joined me. The water rose to my neck. Levi pulled me over to him. His expression pained me, so I kissed his lips and smiled.

"Don't be so upset with them."

"Man, I don't want to talk about them."

Okay," I whispered.

Letting it go, I laid my head on his shoulder. His member poked my leg, growing under me. I glanced at him and he made it jump. He needed his own tension relieved. I could help him with that.

I took the lead and straddled Levi. Looking into his eyes, I lifted, and he guided me down his hard, thick dick. I slowly bounced up and down until I got comfortable with his size. He let out a low groan causing my pussy to get wetter. I placed my hands on his shoulder and picked up the pace.

"Fuck, Sameerah," he groaned, gripping my waist.

His talking made my head a little big. I started bouncing and twerking my ass like it was big. Levi was biting, choking, and kissing all over me as he let me take control. With one of my soapy breasts in his mouth, he slowly inserted a finger in my asshole. The pain, pressure, and pleasure made me cum instantly. I came long and hard, so did Levi... inside of me.

"Damn. You been holdin' back on daddy, Lil' Black Girl," he chuckled. "Gon' fuck around and have my seed planted in you."

"I'm not ready for kids."

"Get on birth control then. I'm lettin' you know now, I ain't pullin' out anymore. Pussy too good for my kids to be all over yo' face."

"Oh, my gosh," I giggled.

My phone buzzing on the sink caught my attention. I let the call ring through, only for it to buzz again. Rolling my eyes, I stepped out to see who it was. It was my mother. I had the right mind not to answer it, but something told me to.

"Hello?"

"Mee Mee, hey. I'm sorry to call, but... I wanted to talk to and see you, so I stopped by your house."

"My house? How do you know where I live?"

"Through the grapevine. I see you're not home, so I was wondering when you would be back? I really need to talk to you. I hate the way things were left off between us."

I removed my phone away from my ear and looked at the

ceiling. I was conflicted. I didn't want to go, but it had to be important knowing she went out her way. Sighing, I pressed the phone back to my ear and agreed.

"Where you goin'?" Levi asked as I stepped in his shower.

"To my old house. My mom is there," I revealed.

"And? She should have called first."

"I know, but I want to hear what she has to say."

"A'ight. It's on you, but you ain't goin' by yo'self."

I nodded in agreement. He let the water out the tub and climbed in the shower with me. Once we finished, we got out, got dressed, and left. I drove my car with Levi in the passenger. My nerves were bad as I thought about what she would say. It damn sure better be something better than last time.

An eerie feeling crept over me as I pulled up to the crib. I saw my mom sitting on the steps of the porch. Gathering myself, I grabbed the handle to get out and so did Levi. I reached over and touched his shoulder to stop him.

"Let me go by myself. We need some privacy, please."

"Fuck that, Sameerah. I don't know yo' moms, so I don't trust her."

"It's cool, Levi. I promise. Roll the window down, if that will make you feel better. I don't think she'll be open if you're around."

Kissing his teeth, he placed two of his guns on his lap and rolled the window down. My mom was looking our way. Levi picked one up and waved it at her. All I could do was shake my head. He was so crazy.

Thanking him, I kissed his cheek and got out. As I approached her, her expression changed. She started shaking her head, mouthing 'no.' Before I could process what was happening, Taizere appeared from behind the house with a gun. He raised it, and I felt a hot, burning sensation fill my chest. Not once, but twice.

My body hit the ground, and as I looked up at the sky, I

heard more gunshots vibrating through my ears. I could hear Levi calling my name, but it was faint. My sight became blurry before going completely dark. The last thing I heard was,

"You can't leave me, Lil' Black Girl. I love you."

To Be Continued...

AFTERWORD

Book 24! I can't believe it's been that many.
This book was so fun to write with AJ. She's my other half and super dope.
We had many emotions writing this book, especially the end!
I hope you enjoyed reading this book as much as we did writing it. We promise to have part two out soon!
We appreciate everyone's support, old and new!
Please, be sure to leave us a review!
Love,
DeeAnn

CONNECT WITH DEEANN:

Facebook 'Personal' Page: Dee Ann
Facebook 'Like' Page: DeeAnn
Reading group: DeeAnn's Readers Den
Twitter: @AuthorDeeAnn_
Instagram: @iam_deeann
Email: authoressdeeann@yahoo.com
Website: iamdeeann.com

ALSO BY DEEANN

There's No Love in a Thug 1-3

When Loving You Goes Wrong 1-2

Two Sides to the Game 1-2 with Ms. Brii

He Can't Love You 1-3

He Can Love You: A Novella

She's Different from the Other Ones 1-5

I'm Falling for a Louisville Savage with Keisha Elle

New Year, New Us: A Louisville Savage New Years' Story with
Keisha Elle

In Love with the King of Memphis 1-3

Coke Gurls: Alabama

If It Wasn't for Your Love: A Novella

AFTERWORD

A note from AJ:

Book #15 is complete, and my first collab! DeeAnn stole what I was going to say so I'll just add: thank you all for reading this, and I hope you all enjoyed reading it as much as we enjoyed writing it. Don't forget to leave reviews!
Love,
AJ

CPSIA information can be obtained
at www.ICGtesting.com
Printed in the USA
LVHW031544120419
613988LV00002B/486